No Time to be Lost

A Screenplay

by

Christopher Yates

Rota Fortunae Press

Milwaukee, Wisconsin

Rota Fortunae Edition 2014

Rota Fortunae is an imprint of Wiseblood Books

www.wisebloodbooks.com

www.wisebloodbooks/rota-fortuna-press

Cover art and illustrations by Dominic Heisdorf

Printed in the United States of America

Set in Arabic Typesetting

Library of Congress
Cataloging-in-Publication Data

Yates, Christopher., 1976-

No Time To Be Lost/ Christopher Yates

1. Yates, Christopher, 1976-screenplay

2. Philosophy and Fiction

ISBN-13: 978-0615924540

ISBN-10: 0615924549

CONTENTS

"There is no time to be lost," Ignatius said sternly. "The apocalypse is near at hand."

—John Kennedy Toole,
A Confederacy of Dunces

Introduction

Everyone knows reading screenplays is absurd. As a literary form, common knowledge has it, they exist only in order to become something else. Which makes them a larval sort of entertainment. Squirmy, prepupal things. When one is published as a book, which is a rare thing indeed, it is only after the movie, or, rather, the *film* it sired sits securely in the cultural consciousness. And even then, one gets the impression that their progenitors are somewhat sheepish about them being in the world like that, somewhat ashamed, as though they'd woken up after a long and regretful night only to be indicted by the evidence of their bad decisions littered all around the room.

When screenplays are read at all, they seem to be read exclusively by people who wish to write them. These are people who always seem to be drunkenly telling you about the one they're working on, spilling their cocktail on your lapel as they outline exactly who will play each character, as they diagram a kind of kinship map, explaining how they know someone who knows someone who knows a producer who, if rightly plied with the proper vice, might read it when they're done. It is the chosen art form, it must be said, of "dreamers."

It is from such people, in such situations, trapped in backyards and cornered in kitchens, that I myself have come to understand just how *hard* it must be to write a screenplay, let alone the whole mystifying business of metamorphosing one into a movie. I mean, a *film*. A screenplay, as I take it, is a lithe and muscled action machine. If at knifepoint I were pressed to name the literary form that is most like a jaguar, it would most certainly be the screenplay. Like that jungle cat, the screenplay doesn't fell its prey with wild abandon, no matter how many car chases or boobs or emoting robots it might have, but stalks its quarry methodically. For a screenplay is an incredibly structured thing, governed by rules as rich and draconian as those that lord over the sestina or the villanelle. They are so complex, in fact, that I suspect there are more books about how to write screenplays than there are published ones to read.

Now then, to borrow a phrase, while we all well know that reading screenplays is absurd, what Christopher Yates's *No Time to be Lost*, a hilarious satire about a band of renegade philosophers drunk on a dream of social justice, presupposes is...maybe it isn't.

Meet your hero, Avery Meir. Philosopher, feminist, Jew. "Promising scholar," one character says of her. "Soon to publish, no doubt." At the story's start, we find her registering for an academic conference, the annual gathering of the Society for Philosophy and Existential Knowledge (SPEK). It's 2010 and we are in St. Augustine, Florida, which is fitting, because everything begins, for the attendees of this conference anyway, with Saint Augustine. Avery is a hive of anxieties when we meet her, having, in the somewhat recent past, finished her dissertation ("Feminism and the Holocaust"), and now frustrated by her lack of opportunities on the job market. Seldom is it that she does not have a cigarette going. She's so anxious that she's incubated an ulcer.

When her advisor, Barrett, a British womanizer, shirks his duties for a more, what, concupiscent imperative, Avery's role at the conference goes from simple networking to introducing the winner of SPEK's Service-Learning medal, Jean-Luc Baptiste, an esteemed French philosopher. The award serves as a species of Macguffin here, something all the characters care about but that we, the audience, don't really—a state of affairs that might cut closer to home than most practicing philosophers, like Yates, would care to admit. For reasons of exposure and publicity, the conference has acquired a sponsor, VidaStout Microbrews, whose eccentric Southern owner, Elmo Exum, is eager for press of his own. Eager, also, for a new liver, which, given how deeply structured a screenplay is, of course comes back to bear on the plot.

As Avery finishes her prefatory remarks, Baptiste, a professorial old man, is conveyed on stage via a wheelchair to accept his medal. With Avery's help he stands behind a podium and delivers a scathing speech, indicting philosophy for becoming a "battle of theories," a pursuit of the privileged, of, in this way, the ignorant. "Who among us has suffered?" he asks, and, to hammer home his point, he plays a video. Faces pass over the screen in a kind of festival of misfortune. Imagine a Save the Children commercial dialed to eleven. While the award's runner-up, Simone Marseilles, watches on in thinly veiled contempt, Baptiste exhorts the crowd to "*Trouvons le plus pauvre des pauvres!,*" to find the very least of these, "the most oppressed, and see with their gaze, speak with their voice." This turns out to be his conclusion, as it were, for he then keels over and dies on stage, in Avery's arms.

Herewith begin the hijinks, the antics. The shenanigans and tomfoolery.

Avery takes Baptiste at his literal word, because, as she says, "He hasn't spoken metaphorically since the '80s." And a loose team forms around the goal of hunting down the most oppressed person in St. Augustine. There's Barrett, his lover, Tanya, and his firearms and Scrabble obsessed TA, Simeon. And then there's the reporter that Exum has sent to cover the conference, Stuart, who also runs VidaStout's after-school program for kids that meets in a bar—"The Pint-Size Scholars."

So much action follows that it's remarkable the story doesn't chafe. The philosophers are quickly thwarted in Florida and, on Exum's dime, head to Paris, where a contretemps with Simone Marseilles forces them to skedaddle, and they beat feet for Myanmar to run down a lead. Meanwhile, Baptiste's mysterious and sudden death has caught the attention of the Feds, of Homeland Security, and they dispatch an agent to investigate. There's a looming scientific establishment of dubious repute and its neighboring nudist colony. There's a helicopter airdrop of a crate of beer and an impromptu exegesis of "Red Dawn"—and, oh, it pains me so to have to write "the original." So far as I know, the script contains the only extant chase scene between a hearse and a couple of mopeds. The thought of Jimmy Carter makes a valiant bid for space on a political philosophy syllabus.

If this all sounds absurd, it's because it is, and delightfully so. *No Time to be Lost* boasts a distinct and distinctive lineage, seeming to take a dram of its inspiration from some of our culture's finest satires. Meir, at once a character and a cipher of sorts, has a literary forbear in Pynchon's Oedipa Maas. The overall sensibility, generally, and certain scenes in particular are redolent of Toole's *A Confederacy of Dunces*, from which the title is taken. Something in the spirit of the narrative is reminiscent of Dave Eggers's first novel, *You Shall Know Our Velocity*. And in its puns and the world-building and the pointed and pithy dialogue, there's a whiff of the Coen brothers.

But *No Time to be Lost* shares something deeper with these other works of the imagination. While it's absurd on the surface, it is deadly serious just below it. Humor, so it goes, allows us to look at ourselves honestly, without despair. And after all is said and even more done, *No Time to be Lost* can be read as an alarm of sorts, a call for a more "authentic" mode of questioning (a character-approved phrasing). The question is not what bored philosophers might be dreaming up at their annual and biannual and semi-annual carnivals of inscrutability—at least it's not exclusively that—but something like what happens to us, as a culture, when we forget how to ask "real" questions at all, when we lose sight of our fundamental duty as humans. That is, given how *farkakte* we've let our culture get, precisely how are we supposed to go about caring for one another? What might that look like? This is a big and scary and serious question, one we should all be paying heed to. And all this from a screenplay, the very least of literary forms.

Cheston Knapp
Nye Beach, Oregon
Winter, 2013

NO TIME TO BE LOST

ACT I

"Vain is the word of that philosopher
which does not heal the suffering of man."
—Epicurean Saying

FADE IN:

Cobalt blue sky over St. Augustine, Florida. Thick white clouds roll slowly by, gradually thickening then dispersing to reveal a 'V' formation of geese vectoring along in geometric bliss.

AVERY (Voice Over)

Someone once said the philosopher's sole aim should be to care about and think about the very things, the *meanings* of things, if you will, that everyday life tends to discourage.

Superimpose:

meaning:

1. something signified; sense.

2. intent; end.

The last of the geese trail away and the sky dissolves into the image of a Viagra advertisement placed aloft on what is revealed to be a plasma billboard.

That's right, discourage.

Beneath the sign the street is filled with fast-moving streams of people. A dark-haired woman in sunglasses tilts her head back and tosses a pill into her throat. Swallows hard. This is AVERY.

AVERY (Voice Over)

Think of traffic or taxes or automated customer service. Think of online dating services or celebrity diet plans, God help us.

Avery hails an approaching taxi.

Think of all that is unthinking or uncaring.

The taxi speeds by, hits a pothole and splashes oily, urban puddle water all over Avery. She fumes.

(Shit!) And ask yourself: what, in all this nonsense, does it mean for the philosopher to pay heed to the unheeded?

A hansom cab carrying a sixty year-old overweight man in a Hawaiian shirt rolls by. This is ELMO EXUM. The cab is drawn by a majestic horse. Avery chases after it with broken heels and a wobbly rolling carry-on bag, desperately waiving a fistful of soggy bills and a debit card.

To listen to the voiceless? To give ear to the unheard?

The hansom cab rolls onward down a busy street, weaving around people. Avery sits facing ELMO. He's wearing a gold crucifix necklace that overlaps his salmon-colored dress shirt, as well as a Red iPod with earphones. He's reading The Financial Times. His white sport-coat is folded over the seat beside him, as is a white cane. Avery adjusts her oil-stained blouse, clears a strand of wet hair from her eyes, then forces an awkward smile. Elmo lowers his newspaper and with a wink offers her the initialed handkerchief from his coat-pocket.

AVERY (Voice Over)

Well, I'm no expert, but here's my take. It means we give a rip.

Curbside of Convention Center. The backpack thuds on the pavement. There is a 'Peace' button affixed to the outer pocket. Avery wraps her fingers around the handle and tugs the bag forward. She marches over a curb toward the entrance of a large hotel, passing by a sleeping HOMELESS MAN and his paltry hat of coins.

Superimpose:

Society for Philosophy and Existential Knowledge (SPEK) Annual Conference.

St. Augustine, Florida

Lobby. Avery's cell-phone rings to the tune of Bob Marley's 'Is This Love?' She draws it from her coat pocket, checks the caller, then slings it to her ear. The chattering of a man's voice crackles through as she stops a few feet from a set of large glass sliding doors.

AVERY

(to phone)

Easy boss. I'm here, man. I'm here.

(beat)

Come again?

Chattering continues as she covers her free ear with her other hand and stares at her own reflection in the doors.

They said that?

She switches the phone to her other hand and throws her now free hand skyward in disbelief.

Can't they at least interview me!?

Shit, man—

The doors' sensor registers and they slide open. She steps forward but the doors close unexpectedly fast, compressing on her trailing bag. She jolts awkwardly, her glasses dropping over the bridge of her nose. A large banner hangs limply across the lobby, reading:

SPEK 2010, St. Augustine!
[Spons. by VidaStout]

A handful of lingering GUESTS stop in conversation to stare at her.

Jesus.

She lowers the phone, turns to face the doors, and gives a resolved two-handed tug on the bag. Suddenly the doors slide open in front of a man and boy entering from the outside. The man is STUART. Avery topples backwards onto the floor.

Stuart is just off the beach, but ready to mix business with pleasure. A camera slung from his shoulder, a shaggy head of blonde tucked under a VidaStout baseball cap, and a "PRESS" notepad tucked into his waistband over a rumpled shirt. The boy is TOMMY, age twelve and expressionless in khaki pants, a cotton sweater-vest over a button-down, parted hair, and a "PRESS" notepad tucked in his waistband.

Stuart and Tommy stop as one, confused by the sight before them.

STUART

Whoa. Here, lemme—

Avery raises her phone-clenching hand in protest.

AVERY

I got it.

Still on her back, she yells in the direction of the concierge desk.

Registration!?

A nearby HOTEL CONCIERGE points the way. Avery stands, brushes herself off, and returns the phone to her ear as she resumes walking. The glass doors close then open again behind Stuart as he watches Avery.

(to phone)

I don't wanna be patient. I wanna be employed. Where the hell are you anyway?!

STUART

on't I know you? Hey hold up

(beat)

C'mon Tommy.

Avery presses on through a larger interior foyer complete with a fountain, open cafe, and people shining shoes. She approaches a conference registration table and turns about.

AVERY

(to phone)

You're kidding me.

Hotel Room. Same time. BARRETT, a fifty-something and self-assured Englishman, reclines on a bed as his attractive young mistress, TANYA, playfully undresses. Sporting a shower cap, he has one hand wrapped around a bottle of massage oil, the other holding the night-stand phone. He places the bottle on a stack of Cambridge Companion texts.

BARRETT

(to phone; British accent)

Yes, well, perhaps you could handle the opening pleasantries. I'm simply indisposed. Prepping.

(beat)

With a student.

(beat)

Simeon? God no. Besides, he's off inking up the freshmen midterms.

Firing Range. Same time. A head of bushy brown hair cranes behind a rifle scope. This is SIMEON. A staccato smattering of semi-automatic shots bursts forth. A tattered string of academic papers hang shredded on distant targets. Simeon raises his head to check his work.

SIMEON

(to himself)

And . . . adios. Good luck on the finals, kids.

He discharges the rifle clip.

Convention Center Foyer. Same time. Avery rubs her temple in distress, with phone at her ear.

AVERY

(to HOSTESS)

Meir, Avery.

Hotel Room. Same time. Tanya applies massage oil to Barrett's hairy chest.

BARRETT

(to Tanya)

Ooh that's cold. . .

(beat, to phone)

Anyway, I know you're up to it, Dr. Meir.
Exude your boundless charm.

Barrett hangs up, reaches for a glass of champagne and smiles coyly at Tanya.

Now now, young lovely.

Convention Center Foyer. Same time. Avery slams the phone down on the registration table. The Hostess is lost in a sea of conference packets.

AVERY

M-E-I-R.

(with sarcasm)

Try the 'unemployed' stack.

Avery checks her Swatch-Watch (with Swatch-Guard) as the Hostess scrambles.

Feck!

She raises her head just as Stuart snaps a photograph of her. He smiles.

STUART

Avery Meir. God almighty.

Avery can't place him, and doesn't care to. Stuart steps forward extending his hand. Avery slides her sunglasses to her forehead and measures the persistent stranger and the boy beside him. Stuart grabs her hand.

It's Stuart. Stuart Macpherson. Yeah. We were on the justice committee together in college. I had that column on sexual health in the paper - you remember, right? I sat in on that philosophy seminar senior year. Yeah. Good times. So—

HOSTESS

Here you are, Dr. Meir.

Avery puts on her reading glasses, half-turns to accept the materials.

STUART

Doctor? Wow. Right on. By the way, wait, don't tell me—

He bridges his fingers over his forehead.

Your thesis was—

Avery pins on her nametag.

AVERY

Feminism and the Holocaust.

(beat)

Pardon me.

She pops a pill in her mouth.

STUART

Right.

He whistles.

Layered. I like it.

(beat, off Tommy)

Oh hey, this is Tommy, part of our career-match enterprise at VidaStout.

No lights are going off for Avery. Stuart tips his cap for emphasis.

The, ahh, the community outreach arm of
the brewery, conference cosponsor. You
probly heard 'bout it.

He motions Tommy over toward Avery and hoists his camera.

Hey! Let's get a quick shot of you two.

He pins a "Pint-Size Scholar" button on Tommy's sweater.

Almost forgot. Welcome to the big
leagues little man.

He shoots photo. Grins and nods.

AVERY

I'm sorry, I—

STUART

Yeah I run this after-school program
down at the pub.

He tussles Tommy's hair. Points to Tommy's button. Avery looks at it with considerable confusion. Tommy snaps a photo of Avery with a small disposable camera.

A little unorthodox maybe. Owner's
a big believer in community service—

AVERY

Um . . .

Stuart pulls out his press notepad.

STUART

—*and* you guys, turns out. Wants me to write up a story on this gig for the corporate newsletter.

Avery, painfully trapped, casts her eyes around the room. Stuart pulls a business card out of his shirt pocket and presents it to her.

Sorry, TMI. But have a go at our website.

He bends down and taps Tommy's press notepad.

Okay, little man. See if you can't go interview some real philosophers!

Stuart gives him a low-five. Tommy turns to Avery for a high-five. Avery obliges awkwardly. Tommy strolls off.

Avery forces a tight smile to Stuart and cinches up her suit jacket.

AVERY

Cute. Um, you know I—

STUART

Good exposure for the kid. Maybe he'll pick up some new three-syllable words.

Avery checks her watch.

AVERY

Feck!

STUART

Or one—

She reaches for her bag handle and packet.

AVERY

Would you excuse me? Have to go make a fool of myself.

She turns briskly and heads for an escalator.

STUART

Yeah, yeah. Hey, we'll catch up later.

(beat)

Watch your step!

(to Hostess)

She looks great, huh. Man, Avery feckin' Meir.

He looks from the Hostess down to the table, and lays eyes on the abandoned phone. He snatches it up and starts off after Avery, his camera bouncing at his side.

¤

Conference Lecture Hall. Avery stands awkwardly at the podium mid-remarks before a sparsely-filled room. Microphone level with her forehead. Her bag stands upright between a nearby table and a handicap ramp to the stage. Tommy is seated Indian-style in a front-row, notepad at the ready. A 'Pint-Size Scholar' balloon is strung high above his chair. Avery clears her throat.

AVERY

. . . delighted to welcome you to this the thirty-second, sorry thirty-third annual week-long convening of the Society for Philosophy and Existential Knowledge.

Stuart bangs through a set of double doors at the rear of the room and clatters his way to a second-row seat. Holding up her phone and pointing a finger, he mouths 'Your Phone.' Avery, expressionless, checks her notes.

If speakers will please keep their remarks
within the allotted time. And if the
audience would please phrase their
comments in the form of questions.

Gentle laughter from the audience. Avery pushes the joke.

No biting. No spitting. And no debates as
to whether Madonna is indeed the
'material girl.'

Sarcastic nod to woman in front row.

Sorry, Judith.

Awkward silence. A loud feedback screech blares through the sound system. Avery wipes her forehead with a sleeve.

An attractive older woman with hair tied back in a tight bun, enters the back of the room with two darkly groomed and European-looking male associates (HENRI and GUY). This is SIMONE. Henri is tall and rail thin with black hair gelled across his forehead, and a small black soul-patch below his bottom lip. Guy is slightly shorter, heavier, and balding, save for long blonde lamb-chop sideburns. They stand with arms folded, revealing anarchy-symbol tattoos across the back of their left hands. Simone's hands are concealed within black leather gloves.

It is my further privilege to welcome Jean-Luc Baptiste, winner of this year's prestigious SPEK Service-Learning medal.

She picks up a yellow post-it note from podium and reads.

Um, jointly sponsored by our generous friends at VidaStout Brewing.

Stuart smiles and gives a little wave to some nearby philosophers.

Right, so, and following Dr. Baptiste's remarks we'll have the further privilege of hearing a response from the runner-up, um—

Checks her program notes.

—Simone Marseilles. Physician, scientist, scholar, and global activist.

Simone obliges a jaw-clenched nod.

So, without further ado, please welcome,
from the Sorbonne, Professor Baptiste.

Applause. Avery retires from the podium and breathes a sigh of relief. Stuart applauds heartily, a pencil between his teeth. Feint applause from the enigmatic trio in the back.

A handsome, silver-haired BAPTISTE approaches the stage in a wheelchair pushed by the Hostess. He motions to stop at the top of the ramp, then points and nods to the 'peace' button on Avery's bag. The Hostess retrieves it and places it on his lapel as the audience watches in collective awe. Tommy snaps a photo. Avery blushes. Stuart snaps a photo and gives Avery a thumbs-up.

Avery and the Hostess help Baptiste stand at the podium. Avery places a necklace-medal about his neck, then takes her seat at the nearby table. Baptiste steadies himself, a sharp gleam in his eye.

Guy whispers something to Simone, who smirks. She fingers her blouse, as if imagining the feel of the medal.

BAPTISTE

(in accented English)

Men and women, to you I say 'peace.'
Once, with a shudder in our voice, we
philosophers spoke of peace, of justice.

He turns aside and coughs loudly. Audience members look at one another in slight confusion. Baptiste sways uneasily and grips the podium with both hands. The room darkens slightly, as if cued, and a video slide-show begins behind Baptiste. It contains an array of images juxtaposing global strife, war, and hunger with images of universities and books.

Philosophy today, you see, is a broken
family. A battle of theories.

He mops his sweaty brow.

Empiricism vies with rationalism, critique
with science, the mind with the body,
America with Europe. We stand engaged
in a tug-of-war, do we not?

He pauses dizzily and takes a sip of water. Guy smirks and chuckles. Simone shushes him. Avery's face is bathed in the light from the video images. Baptiste gestures toward the video screen.

And meanwhile there is famine, rape,
hunger. What does philosophy have to
say to these? Who among us has suffered?

Stuart rushes to write down every word.

No, we are persons of privilege, and our theories, our systems—these are the currency of privilege. Can we break free of this academic economy? Can we hear the cry of the oppressed?

He pauses and raises his arms with the question.

I confess we cannot, and yet we must. To whom then do we turn to regain our lost footing? Who is impartial? Who hungers most for justice?

(steadying beat)

Where hides the mind with a pure conscience?

The video lingers on a shot of a Mexican woman raising a child up over a border fence.

The mind that can call our minds away from ideology—

Simone looks on with contempt.

—and back to their social duty?

SIMONE

(quietly, hint of sarcasm)

Here comes the blessed dream.

BAPTISTE

You see, if philosophy, if peace is to flourish, we must be vigilant. Leaving no stone unturned. Here, now, this very week, we must enact a global enterprise to find our voice, our vision.

The video freezes on a shot of protestors at the U.S. Capitol Building. Baptiste coughs and waves a finger.

Indeed, as those before us have said, we must—

He raises a thundering fist.

—*trouvons le plus pauvre des pauvres!* The most oppressed, and see with their gaze, speak with their voice.

He teeters to one side, coughs hard, struggles to wipe his forehead with a handkerchief. Avery looks at Baptiste then the Hostess with concern.

In Myanmar, you see, a young man I know, a bright light . . .

He is overtaken by dizziness and gasping. He begins to teeter then collapses in the direction of Avery. She braces him and lowers him to the floor. He grasps her hand tightly and locks eyes with her before expiring on the floor.

Freeze-Frame on Avery's shocked face.

AVERY (Voice Over)

The thing of it is, every once in a while something comes along that *blurs all the lines . . .*

Hotel balcony. Same time. Barrett, donning a plush white robe (with conference name-tag dutifully affixed), stands on a balcony outside his love nest, a long-tipped cigarillo between his teeth. He draws a gold lighter from the robe pocket. The plasma billboard sharpens into an advertisement depicting a multi-ethnic gathering of happy picknickers and the slogan: "Carpe Vida, By VidaStout Microbrews."

AVERY (Voice Over)

. . . Poetry and thought. Life and death. Research and relevance. I think you know what I'm talking about.

Barrett thumbs the lighter into a sparking flame.

Conference hall. Same time. Stuart's camera flashes. Avery's eyes freeze and stare back at him, then past him to Simone as she exits the room, then finally down upon Baptiste's face now cradled in her arms, and the 'Peace' button on his lapel.

AVERY (Voice Over)

. . . Anyway, and there you are, caught in this web of God knows what. And you think to yourself, as I thought to myself: If A, then B. If B, then, well, scholar, what next?

Dissolve to view of U.S. Capitol Building at night. Then to interior of Washington, DC office, day. A handsome late middle-aged man, sits at his desk before a large window with the Capitol Building. This is AGENT CAVELL. His sleeves are rolled up and he is attempting to balance paperclips, pens, and a stick of gum on the scales of a desktop figure of lady justice. A nearby name-plate reads: 'Agent James Cavell. Intelligence Liaison'.

An assistant, HOWIE, packs up photographs and books from a nearby bookcase.

HOWIE

So long security reports, *History of Riot Response*, Dulles biography . . . You know, sir, say what you will about early retirement,

Wiping dust off a book.

Cold-War Armaments . . . I still don't see why, you know, why now?

He drops a stack of books in a box then pauses, beholding an antique sword on the shelf. Agent Cavell achieves momentary balance on the scales and leans back in satisfaction. Takes a picture of the scales with his cell-phone.

AGENT CAVELL

Not retiring, Howie. Just moving into the private sector.

Howie brandishes the sword.

HOWIE

But, sir, you wrote the book on homeland security. You're one promotion away from full clearance.

He looks down the length of the blade toward Agent Cavell.

Could be playing golf with the Joint
Chiefs in another five years.

Agent Cavell nods to the sword.

AGENT CAVELL

Careful with that.

An older gentleman, CHIEF, enters sporting a cheap suit and a file-folder. Howie turns and Chief frowns at the tip of the sword. Clears his throat.

CHIEF

Got a minute, Jim?

Howie dutifully hands Chief the sword and bows out of the room. Chief drops the file folder on the desk.

How 'bout one more, for the road?

The scales tip unevenly. Agent Cavell pops the stick of gum in his mouth and crosses his hands behind his head. Eyes the window.

AGENT CAVELL

Another dinner with the Saudis? Nah, let someone else have a go.

CHIEF

This one's a little more recreational. University types. Possible foul-play. Didn't you do philosophy at Georgetown?

AGENT CAVELL

Uh-huh. But I was also an anarchist then.

He swings his chair around to face Chief. Chief breathes carefully on the blade.

CHIEF

Perfect.

He delicately opens file with the blade tip, revealing a photograph of Baptiste.

'Cause when a much beloved French-Algerian scholar in seemingly perfect health hits the floor in an American lecture hall, well, that's exactly what we got.

He lays the sword across the desk and turns for the door. Agent Cavell fiddles with the scales.

AGENT CAVELL

So why not let Customs handle it?

Chief pauses at the door, his hand on the knob.

CHIEF

(cryptically)

'Cause he wasn't on Customs' payroll in the eighties.

Agent Cavell turns around and gives Chief a measuring glance.

Would get you out of town, Jim. Give it some thought.

(beat)

Plane leaves tonight.

Nods to the scales.

Never understood the blindfold.

AGENT CAVELL

Impartiality.

CHIEF

Hmmpff.

Chief exits, whistling a tune. Agent Cavell eyes the folder and sighs. He lets his gaze carry over to a stack of books. Something catches his eye. He stands up and walks to the stack, retrieving a dusty edition of Plato's Republic *from the top, and holds it pensively.*

¤

Convention Center Parking Lot. Evening. The plasma billboard dissolves into a scene of a man and woman drinking bottled water on a scenic sand dune. The following slogan underscores the image in cursive: "Elan Vital, Water For Life."

Pigeons take flight from the billboard's steel structure.

Convention Center Reception on Elevated Patio. Evening. Pigeons land on an ocean-side ledge behind Avery. She's seated on the brick patio, smoking a cigarette. Conferencegoers mingle about in slightly-subdued mood, swapping stories and chatting over drinks. Avery ashes her cigarette into a large potted plant where a fat ceramic seagull is perched, 'watching' her.

Stuart approaches with drinks in hand through a set of double doors leading to the patio. Press notepad tucked in his waistband. He pauses as Baptiste's body is wheeled by on a gurney, then makes his way through the crowd and across the patio. He hunkers down beside Avery and offers a drink.

STUART

You were a Jack-n-Coke girl, right?

Avery skeptically takes the drink. Stuart makes a kissing noise to the ceramic seagull and cheers his own drink. Avery mouths a cigarette. Stuart produces a lighter.

Simone and her associates linger across the patio. Guy sips an espresso and mans a camcorder, surveying the festivities. Henri takes notes in a black notebook as Simone, gazing toward the water, dictates.

AVERY

Hey, so weren't you the one that gave the presentation on the *Nausea* novel in our Sartre seminar with Dr. B?

Stuart opens up his notepad.

STUART

Wow. Yeah. Guilty.

(beat)

'Existentialism as Gastric-Bypass.'

AVERY

God. I wanted to kill myself after that.

Stuart nods solemnly then swigs his VidaStout beer. He catches sight of a VidaStout Beer advertisement on the distant plasma billboard. Smiles, raises his own bottle.

STUART

Boo-yah!

Avery takes no interest. She then notices a HOTEL MAID struggling to sweep up some broken glass. Getting back on topic,

AVERY

Thing is, I have to say he had me man. He was genius. Beautiful, ya know? Then he kicks it.

She takes a drag and leans her head back. The Hotel Maid is accidentally knocked from behind by a conference attendee and cuts her hand on a piece of glass.

STUART

Sartre?

AVERY

Baptiste, bro.

Stuart attempts, badly, to blow smoke rings.

STUART

Ahh. Right. Heavy. Hey does this place have a hot-tub?

AVERY

Shit, I should have studied with him, you know?

STUART

Yep.

AVERY

Trouvons les plus pauvre des pauvres.

Stuart nods dumbly and fingers the rim of his bottle.

STUART

Hey, you should come down to the pub some time! Meet the kids.

AVERY

(translating)

Find the very least of these.

She takes a glance skyward at the stars.

The most oppressed, and see with their gaze, speak with their voice.

A splotch of blood stains the Hotel Maid's uniform. The MANAGER tries to maintain a public smile, but he is visibly infuriated at her carelessness. Stuart nods a sip down and wipes his mouth.

STUART

Wow. That'll copy.

(beat)

'Course, I'm not sure your everyday Floridian could—

AVERY

I dunno, man. Maybe it's shit. But it felt like something more, something real.

She flicks a cigarette butt back behind her over the ledge, scaring off the pigeons.

No. Gimme a cigarette. It means what it means. Has to.

Stuart nods.

He hasn't spoken metaphorically since the '80s.

Barrett approaches with a smirk on his face and Tanya on his arm. He tugs over a chaise lounge just as another conference-goer is about to sit in it. Reclining, legs crossed,

BARRETT

Helluva way to start, darling, killing off the keynote. Tanya, fetch us a gin and tonic, love, thank you.

Tanya playfully kisses his head.

TANYA

(British accent)

Don't overdo it, handsome. We've still footnotes to format.

Barrett raises his eyebrows. Tanya exits.

AVERY

Go feck yourself, Barrett. And feck the Sorbonne for not hiring me.

Stuart wipes his palms on his pants.

STUART

Howdy Dr. B. Long time.

He leans over to shake hands.

AVERY

You remember Stuart MacPherson. Sat in on your seminar our senior year. Here with the sponsor to do up a little news story on all this.

BARRETT

Of course. Of course. But, one might have to parlay it into an obit piece at this point.

Avery crunches ice.

Now, now. It's tragic. It's Shakespeare.

He gestures about.

But the man had a whole system devoted to human finitude. Seems fitting in a way.

AVERY

. . . see with their gaze, speak with—

BARRETT

Yes, yes. Well, people say all kinds of things on their deathbed. He's just lucky he didn't have to endure the Q'n'A.

He slurps his drink. Avery watches as the Hotel Maid, clearly having a bad night, finishes cleaning up the glass only to be handed an armful of empty glasses by another attendee.

Barrett mats his forehead with a white handkerchief. Lights a cigarillo.

Now, I'll allow we need the evocative in this business. And, truth be told, we need the SPEK medal to keep things lively. Which brings me to a further point—

Tanya approaches with drinks. Barrett freezes at the sight of Simone and her associates. In quiet alarm,

Oh sweet Moses.

Avery and Stuart look at each other. Barrett fumbles for words. Henri lights a cigarette for Simone while Guy stands ready with an ashtray for the match.

STUART

They with the dead guy?

Avery spits a piece of ice in her glass. Drops the conference program in his lap.

AVERY

Simone—

BARRETT

—Marseilles. The savvyest siren of the lot. Heir apparent on the French scene, so it seems. Turning her work toward applied ethics, they say. Widows and gypsies and other sparkling causes. My my.

AVERY

Anyway, what further point, B?

Barrett's eyes are stuck on Simone.

BARRETT

We did our graduate work together at Berkley. Marx, Freud, Nietzsche.

(beat)

Bedeviling hoax of my dreams, she was. Stirred up the polis and such together for a time.

Dissolve to Shipping Yard. Night. A younger Simone, dressed in army fatigues, listens with a stethoscope to the steel wall of a shipping container. She nods to a nearby HIPPIE-LOOKING MAN who then breaks open the container with a crow-bar. A dozen cowering ASIAN IMMIGRANTS stream out of the container. Nearby ACTIVISTS hand them bundles of food and clothing. A younger Barrett, pasty-legged in khaki shorts and a polo shirt, blares at them through a megaphone to the consternation of Simone.

BARRETT

Welcome to America!

Return to scene. Simone eyes Barrett from across the patio and begins walking his way. Guy and Henri linger at their post, toying with the camcorder.

TANYA

They're looking very Euro for philosophers. Existentialists?

Barrett forces an awkward smile in Simone's direction.

BARRETT

(sotto)

Behold. The Parisian Reds.

Swigs his drink.

AVERY

B, point two?

BARRETT

Eh? Oh, they're to reissue the medal by week's end. Replacement keynote, the works.

Simone saunters his way, poised with a constructed smile toward times gone by.

Madame ladyship, ever a pleasure.

He kisses her hand. She exhales and offers her cheek. With a formal kiss,

How's the revolution?

Avery rolls her eyes. Stuart pockets his IPhone and snaps the cover off his camera.

My condolences concerning Jean-Luc. I'm sure he was an inspiration.

SIMONE

(in accented English)

Ahh, yes, a tragedy. Just as his work was beginning to ripen.

Stuart clears his throat and tips his hat to Simone.

STUART

Hiya. Stuart MacPherson.

He taps his pencil on his notepad.

Doing up a story on this shin-dig. I wonder if—

AVERY

(to Barrett)

They're re-issuing the medal?! To who?

Simone turns toward her abruptly.

BARRETT

Ahem. Darling, meet Avery Meir. Oppressed woman and Jew. Promising scholar. Soon to publish, no doubt.

Avery and Simone nod coolly to one another. Stuart vies for Simone's attention.

STUART

So, you, you're also into this least-of-these thing—I mean, ah, these outside-curricular type deals? I do a bit of volunteering myself, actually. So—

Barrett folds his arms awkwardly and nods nearby to the beleaguered Hotel Maid for another drink. Confused, the order doesn't register.

BARRETT

Now now. Let's not, well, we all have our charity work of course but the Mademoiselle here will—

Simone lays a hand on Barrett's shoulder.

SIMONE

—We do what we can, as you know. Nothing more. Plain service is labor enough.

Avery's phone rings ('Is this love . . . ?') in Stuart's shirt pocket. She looks around, confused. Stuart looks down at his chest. Avery grabs the phone from his shirt.

AVERY

Pardon me.

She turns aside and takes the call.

STUART

Anyway, so, your projects? Your message to the masses? Wonder if I could get a quote here.

SIMONE

(evasively)

Oh young man, I wouldn't know where to begin. I have much to learn myself, you see, but with our medical and development initiatives there's hardly the time. After all, it's one thing to interpret the world, but still another to change it, don't you think? Put that in your paper if you like. Perhaps there shall be more to discuss in the coming days.

She turns to Barrett.

I must rest. So much to process. And the relief work in the Sudan took it out of me I'm afraid.

Avery snaps her phone shut and rejoins the group. She fishes for a cigarette but is all out.

AVERY

EMTs. Need me to ID the body.

SIMONE

Ahhh. Of course. Here,

She hands Avery a half-smoked cigarette.

I'll manage it. You enjoy your fun.

Avery stands awkwardly with Simone's cigarette. Simone turns to Barrett.

Goodbye old friend.

She kisses his cheek

All the best in your teaching and writing.

(to the group)

Adieu.

She exits back across the patio. Barrett looks after her, jingling change in his pocket.

AVERY

Bitch.

BARRETT

Easy now, dear. Forget not your feminisisms.

Avery shakes her head and takes a fresh smoke from Stuart.

AVERY

C'mon. She's got a sleeve as long as the Nile. Not to mention tenure at two universities, endless sabbaticals to traipse around the world.

Ditches Simone's cigarette

Feckin' menthols.

Stuart looks from Avery to Barrett. Tanya stoops down to snap a picture of the ceramic seagull with a disposable camera. Barrett considers the point.

BARRETT

Good God. She was a touch sly wasn't she?

He pauses and feels his just-kissed cheek; resolved.

Damn. Still fancies herself a friend of the proletariat.

(beat)

Likely be draped in Baptiste's medal by week's end. Well, double damn.

He takes a drink and turns to the ocean view. Stuart makes notes on his press-pad.

STUART

Wow. This might even make the wire.

Avery throws him a cold stare.

What? It's news.

Barrett turns around.

BARRETT

Say again, lad?

Stuart thumps his notebook.

STUART

Academic activists. You know, news. Plus, alliteration!

Avery sees Barrett's eyes widen with thought. Beat.

AVERY

Oh, hey, nah-ah B.

Barrett grunts and leans pensively against the patio ledge, eyes on the great sea and the traffic lights of St. Augustine.

BARRETT

Behold, the republic of swine. Injustice, strife.

Tanya rubs his shoulder in comfort. Stuart looks at Avery in confusion.

AVERY

Look, man—

BARRETT

And here we are, paralyzed by the prophet's words. You said it yourself.

AVERY

Hang on. I never—

BARRETT

Ahh, tsk tsk.

AVERY

So, so what then?! You wanna round up some homeless dudes and drop some Kant on'em?! I mean—

Barrett gestures toward the city.

BARRETT

A touch of social relevance, professor. A few days while the medal hangs in the balance. A little field work. You're a good liberal, why not—

AVERY

Okay. One, it's naive and reckless. Two, it's offensive and manipulative.

She ashes a cigarette on the ceramic seagull. Stuart does a double-take at the 'bird'.

Social justice isn't some *game*, man. I know, I work in 'marginal theory', remember?

Barrett exhales dramatically. He fiddles with his drink and swats some flies.

BARRETT

Indeed. You and our French colleagues, so it seems.

AVERY

What in God's name are we gonna do?
Quit teaching? Join the Peace Corps?
Seriously.

BARRETT

Hmmm.

Stuart grins, loving it. Avery pauses, somewhat flabbergasted, and lights a smoke. She looks over the cigarette at Barrett. Beat. She flicks the lighter shut.

AVERY

You're ser—

BARRETT

Aye.

AVERY

Here? Now? We ditch the conference and
start saving the world?

BARRETT

Hmm.

Barrett strokes his chin in thought, wide-eyed. Avery tilts her head back against the ledge and takes a deep breath. Stuart twiddles a pencil between his fingers.

STUART

Would make one helluva story.

Barrett nods and raises his glass. Avery clamps her hands over her eyes.

AVERY

No. No no no no.

Barrett takes a seat beside her.

BARRETT

Humanitarianism on the streets. A moral compass for the mind. Mere justice loosed upon the convention—

Avery shovels a pill down her throat.

AVERY

Jesus. My ulcer's flaring. I'm going to the library.

She gets up to exit, hands her glass to Stuart, and casts a sneering look in the direction of Guy and Henri.

BARRETT

(yelling)

Picture it on your dossier, professor! If not now—

She ignores him. Making her way across the patio toward the reentry doors, her bag in tow, she passes the Hotel Maid, who, with gauze wrapped around her finger, carefully dusts lint from Baptiste's sport-coat before placing it on a hanger.

HOTEL MAID

(to herself)

Con Dios, Señor?

The 'Peace' button glimmers in the moonlight. Avery stops, tilts her head back for a deep breath, then turns around and meets the plaintive gazes of Barrett and Stuart. Barrett blows a smoke ring and raises his eyebrows.

Convention Center Foyer. The group hops the down escalator.

AVERY

(facing group)

We give it a go. We do some prep work. Then we go local. Then we report our findings here before the Baptiste memorial.

She checks her watch. Tanya applauds.

Seventy two hours. Nothing fancy, B. Just good, honest Aristotelian activism, medal or no medal.

Barrett helps himself to a drink from a server headed on the adjacent 'up' escalator. Nods solemnly.

BARRETT

Marvelous.

They step off the escalator and move through the lobby.

And of course we'll need an issue to petition, chants, clipboards—

AVERY

Lord.

Elmo Exum, same garb, same newspaper, is perched atop a shoeshine chair in the background in the lobby. Tommy is seated in the chair next to him, reading his own Financial Times.

Outside Convention Center Entrance. Night. Same time. A black hearse screeches to a halt, curbside. Simeon, lately of the shooting range, steps out the driver's side in a cloud of smoke and flashes a 'peace' sign toward the group as they begin to pile in. He's wearing a black t-shirt that reads: 'Caution: This Vehicle Makes Wide Right Turns.' He pops the trunk and hoists their bags in.

EMT's wheel Baptiste's body behind the group toward a waiting ambulance. Stuart shakes his head in amusement at the hearse, then takes a thoughtful glance over the hearse at the sheet-covered body. Simone has a solemn word with the EMTs and signs a clipboard. Simone beholds the hearse then looks upward slyly before returning toward the lobby.

On a Patio overlooking the entrance, Guy, and Henri observe the departure and Simone's cue. Guy, with camcorder hanging from his shoulder, smiles deviously, then hands a small GPS tracking device to Henri. Henri inserts the device in a wad of chewing gum, then leans over and spits it on the top of the hearse.

ACT II

"All great deeds and all great thoughts
have a ridiculous beginning."
—Albert Camus

FADE IN:

St. Augustine Airport. Night. There is the roar of a jet engine as an airplane touches down on the runway.

Convention Center Hallway. The Hotel Concierge slides an electronic master-key-card into the lock on a hotel bedroom door. A gum-chewing Agent Cavell steps past him, entering the room. The Hotel Concierge flicks on the lights.

HOTEL CONCIERGE

I'll send housekeeping by in an hour or so to collect his personal affects.

AGENT CAVELL

Thanks. And, listen, I'll have a look at the guest list if you don't mind.

HOTEL CONCIERGE

Certainly, officer.

Agent Cavell takes a few slow steps then sets down his briefcase, and snaps on a pair of latex gloves. The room is in neat order. A travel-picture of Baptiste with a woman, presumably his wife, adorns the dresser. He shoots a few photos with his cell-phone camera. He places his hands on his hips and scans the room for something, anything of interest. On a table in the corner of room rests a small stack of folders and a book. Two coffee cups stand adjacent to these. He observes the mugs are stained with the remnants of coffee. He smells the mugs, then carefully swabs samples of their contents. Takes picture.

Turning to the book, he notices it is a first edition of Das Kapital, *by Karl Marx. Opening it, he finds the following inscription: "To Jean-Luc, with admiration. SM." He holds a finger on the page.*

AGENT CAVELL

SM.

He exhales then shovels the text into a zip lock bag and lobs it to his briefcase. A punctuated blaring pulses through the room. He turns about then steps over to silence the night-stand alarm clock. He discovers a small leather date-book. He opens it carefully and a photograph drops to the floor. He studies a picture of Baptiste shaking hands with a man wearing a ski mask and the gun-slinging garb of a guerrilla fighter. He turns it over to find the faded initials "ST" scrawled on the back.

He looks across the room to his briefcase and the freshly-bagged book. He scratches his chin, looks down at the photo again. Holds the initialed side under the lamp.

SM, ST. ST . . .

He exhales and tosses the photo toward his briefcase.

Looks like we're just gettin' warmed-up, Chief.

Meanwhile around St. Augustine:

Athletic Track/Field. Day. Avery runs steadily around a track, a Camelback strapped round her shoulders. Stuart, sporting his VidaStout cap, blissfully follows close behind. Barrett trails them, weaving about on a rickety bicycle while barking an indeterminable cadence through a megaphone. Simeon sits on a folding chair beside the track and mans a cardboard table containing an assortment of 'Elan Vital' bottled waters, as well as PowerGel snack treats. Tommy is beside him reading a book by Sartre. A 'Blondes Do it Better' T-shirt hangs over Simeon's pudgy belly as he looks intently at a Scrabble board then yawns as the others pass by. Avery sucks intently on her Camelback tube.

Guy, straddling a moped in a nearby parking lot and unseen by the group, sucks on a Slurpee. Nearby Henri monitors their track training through binoculars. Henri lowers the field glasses, ponders the situation, then meets Guy's glance with an ambivalent shoulder-shrug. Guy offers him some Slurpee.

Ropes Course Challenge Wall. Day. Avery throws her elbows over the top of a ropes-course wall and tugs herself up to the platform. Simeon sits casually atop the wall with Monadology *by the philosopher, Leibniz, in hand. An image of Che Guevera adorns his T-shirt. He gives Avery a thumbs-up. Avery repositions herself atop the wall and catches her breath. She stands, turns with her back to Stuart and Barrett down below, then trust-falls down toward their cradling arms.*

College Classroom. Day. Stuart catches a multi-colored Rubix-Cube then looks up intently at Avery, who stands before the group, pointer in hand as though lecturing. On the chalkboard behind her is written: "The Local Cost of Globalization." Simeon and Barrett engage in a covert game of Scrabble between nearby desks. Avery nods to Stuart as if to say 'the floor is yours.'

College Classroom. Night. Stuart presents a slideshow, with "Stuart M: Third-World Diseases" scrawled on the chalkboard. Avery tosses a pill into her mouth, and kicks Barrett's desk to jolt him awake. Simeon grabs a buzzing fly in his fist.

College Chemistry Lab. Night. A safety-goggled Simeon tugs on a long synthetic line and explodes a make-shift pipe-bomb. A cloud of smoke rises and covers Avery, Stuart, and Barrett. Sprinklers shower water upon the group.

College Quad. Day. Shakespeare's The Merchant of Venice *is cradled in Barrett's lap as thunder booms and rain falls off an oversized umbrella. Avery, Stuart, and Simeon, with photo-copies in hand, begrudgingly read character parts as Barrett directs the action with a pointer. Avery sips green-tea from a mason jar. Concealed on a nearby knoll, with mopeds parked nearby, Henri and Guy covertly observe the group. Henri, binoculars poised, swats bitterly at a mosquito. Guy offers him some Twizzlers. Taking one, Henri tears off a bite then lowers the glasses. He motions to Guy for a cell-phone, then catches it and dials a number.*

HENRI

(in French; subtitled)

The capitalists are organizing.

Guy looks on with a snort and sinister smile.

Dissolve to College Classroom. Night. The hands of Avery (Swatch-Watch), Stuart, Barrett, and Simeon slide together in team formation atop a desk with an 8x10 photo of Baptiste resting on it.

ALL

Justice!

Their hands push downward and out.

¤

Convention Center Concierge Desk. Day. Agent Cavell stands at the counter chewing gum and examines the conference guest list. Baptiste's date-book rests nearby, as does The Republic, *a few post-it notes stuck to its pages. The HOTEL CONCIERGE is across the counter from Agent Cavell, trying to load something up on a computer. On the wall behind the counter a row of clocks display differing times around the globe.*

High heels click on the marble nearby as Simone approaches the desk and lays some paperwork on the counter. The Hotel Concierge pivots the computer monitor so that Agent Cavell can see it. Security camera footage from the last couple of days begins to play.

HOTEL CONCIERGE

More faxes, Madamoiselle?

SIMONE

Yes, please. And this.

She positions a cardboard placard atop the counter. It is an invitation to make gifts "in honor of Baptiste's life" to a list of "charities" around the world. The Concierge nods in approval. Simone looks past him and sees another ATTENDANT carefully placing the SPEK Medal in the hotel safe. Her eyes glimmer. The Concierge preps Simone's paperwork atop the fax machine.

HOTEL CONCIERGE

One moment.

On the computer monitor, Avery is giving her introductory remarks. Agent Cavell looks up from the monitor to discover that Simone, her back leaned against the counter, is observing him. She nods to his copy of The Republic.

SIMONE

(in accented English)

A student of philosophy?

He looks from her to the book.

AGENT CAVELL

Me? No. Well, not intentionally.

Simone measures him somewhat seductively with her gaze. Cavell focuses on the security footage, then back on Simone. He offers his hand.

Jim Cavell. Homeland Security.

A tremor flashes over Simone's face. She recovers quickly and takes his hand.

SIMONE

Simone.

With coquettish smile.

Philosophe provocateur.

Cavell pauses awkwardly. He looks at the "donations" placard.

I trust you've heard of our misfortune?

Cavell handles the sign more closely. On the nearby monitor Baptiste is delivering his address.

He was a brave, mysterious man.

The Hotel Concierge places Simone's paperwork on the counter and nods. Simone collects it.

But I didn't realize he was of security
interest.

AGENT CAVELL

Everything's of interest in my line.

She brushes a bit of lint off his coat sleeve, lingering,

SIMONE

Well, we have something in common then.

AGENT CAVELL

That so?

She runs her hand down his sleeve then rests her palm on the counter.

SIMONE

In your line of work, suspicion is a skill rather than a pathology. My colleagues say I'm impossibly suspicious.

She nods to the computer monitor. It plays footage of Simone interacting with Barrett, Avery, and Stuart on the Hotel patio.

But then again, I know them too well.

Agent Cavell follows her glance to the monitor.

AGENT CAVELL

Ahh. A predicament.

SIMONE

So it is.

She collects her paperwork and pats The Republic.

Bonne chance with your reading.

She kisses his cheek politely, then whispers in his ear.

Mind you, it's mostly bullshit.

Agent Cavell holds the moment in the balance, then reaches into his wallet.

AGENT CAVELL

Hang on.

He presents her with a business card.

Here. In case. Well, in case Customs gives you any trouble.

Simone accepts the card, bows slightly, and turns away. She approaches the large foyer, her hand clenched tightly on the card as she reaches a courtesy phone. All business. Agent Cavell retrains his focus on the computer monitor and guest list.

¤

Warehouse/Factory. Day. Barrett has driving goggles on his forehead and a cigarillo in his mouth. He cranes his head against the grimy glass of a broken window. Tanya stands beside him on a cinder-block and idly paints her nails. Inside a crowd of LABORERS run fabric through sewing machines.

BARRETT

Good to be in the field again.

Tanya slips.

Mind the gap, love.

Simeon's Hearse. Same time. Simeon and Avery pull out from the university campus. Simeon is sucking on a hookah-pipe hose. The hookah is bungee-strapped to the front console of the hearse. Smoke wafts through the car.

Avery, Sharpie in hand, pours over a newspaper for any indications of local social injustice. She coughs.

SIMEON

Any likely suspects?

He starts to lower the windows to clear the smoke. The newspaper rattles chaotically in Avery's lap.

AVERY

Dude!

The City page flattens across her face. She tears it away, then stops, looking at a headline.

Dude.

Simeon offers her the hose.

Warehouse/Factory. Same time. Doors burst open. A cinder-block lands on the dusty floor. Coughing sounds from behind the cloud of dust. Barrett pushes through with Tanya close behind waving a map at the dust. Assorted laborers look up, confused. Shouting outside. Barrett grunts and deftly wraps his cardigan around the neck of an approaching FOREMAN. He nods in the direction of a fusebox.

BARRETT

The switch, my love.

Tanya flips down a crank and the power shuts down. The machines stop. Everything goes dark. An alarm blares. Barrett struggles with his captive.

In the name of the Least of These, of Abe Lincoln, and Lady Thatcher, I hereby proclaim this a day of emancipation!

The workers are motionless.

Emancipation!

The Foreman flips Barrett to the floor. Workers scatter in a frenzy. Tanya, screaming in mixed fear/euphoria rushes to gather up piles of garments.

Simeon's Hearse. Same time. The hearse cruises past the warehouse as the alarm blares outside. Suddenly a panicked Tanya scampers in front of the hearse with an armful of clothing. Avery looks up as Simeon hits the brakes. They stare.

AVERY

Oh boy.

Simeon observes Tanya's frenzied sprint.

SIMEON

Whoa.

Avery shakes her head in frustration, then plants her finger on a map.

AVERY

Hop on the freeway.

Convention Center Hotel Room. An electronic key card slides in and out of a room door. Agent Cavell enters past the Hotel Concierge. This is the room in which Barrett and Tanya preoccupied themselves. Agent Cavell snaps on the latex gloves and has a quick look around. Squatting beside the bed, he snaps a small bubble of chewing gum then carefully retrieves the shower-cap and massage oil. He takes a cell-phone photo then files them away in a ziplock bag.

He turns and approaches the balcony curtains, drawing them back with a pen. The Hotel Concierge impatiently checks his watch. Cavell steps out onto the balcony. A few floors down is the pool area. Stuart looks around suspiciously then hops the fence into the pool area and heads for the hot-tub. Agent Cavell squints at him. He knows the face from somewhere. Stuart settles into the tub and begins jotting notes in his notepad. Cavell shoots a picture of him and shakes his head.

HOTEL CONCIERGE

Was there anything else you—

Agent Cavell steps back through the curtains.

AGENT CAVELL

I'll need a look at the phone log. But, maybe more importantly, did you happen to notice anything unusual about the Baptiste character, or any of the other guests?

The Hotel Concierge straightens his shirt-cuffs beneath his sport-coat.

HOTEL CONCIERGE

Well, they're academics.

AGENT CAVEL

Right.

(beat)

Anyone else check out early or, I dunno, seem a bit out of place?

Simeon's Hearse. Backroads. Day. Avery looks up from her map. Checks a washed out turn-off.

AVERY

Here we go. Swing a right.

Simeon careens through a tight turn. Takes a pull on the hose. Avery steadies herself and has another look at the newspaper.

SIMEON

Talk to me.

Avery holds up the newspaper. A black circle has been drawn around a headline.

AVERY

'Life on the Margins: Bare Republic's
Embodied Protest'

SIMEON

Sounds promising.

Avery looks around the dashboard space.

AVERY

You got a GPS?

Simeon clears his throat and spits into the window. Rolls it down and flicks at the phlegm.

SIMEON

I'm like a bloodhound. Sorta favored that way.

He snorts and guns the hearse through a four-way stop. Avery checks the play in her lap-belt. After a few blocks she spots a dilapidated sign that reads "Bare Republic Community of Peace."

AVERY

Dude!

Simeon fishtails up the drive and comes to a halt at the back of an old lodge. They both take an uncertain look around.

SIMEON

Wonder if they got a firing range.

Dissolve to Bare Republic deck. Day. Avery stands before a sixty-something and completely naked man with a gray ponytail and a pink visor. This is KERT. He is leaning on a porch-rail, sipping Orangina through a straw. Simeon engages a NAKED WOMAN in Scrabble.

KERT

And when the homeowners society linked arms with the DA's office we skedaddled to this little piece of remote park-land.

He looks around, indicating the property.

A former convent actually.

Avery gulps.

Pretty sweet.

He looks around the landscape again. Smoke billows from rooftop vents in the distance. Avery shields her eyes from the sun.

AVERY

What's that, the monastery?

KERT

Monad Labs. Medical research, local health clinic, so they claim. But more of a chop-shop for human organs. My theory anyhow. Prey on everyone, especially the uninsured. I keep calling the Feds on'em but—

AVERY

Nice to have neighbors.

Simeon ponders the Scrabble board and nods.

SIMEON

'Pen-Ultimate.' Okay, that's cool. I can hang with modifiers.

Kert sets his drink down and pushes off the rail.

KERT

Anyway. C'mon, I'll introduce you to the other guardians.

He stops and turns to Avery.

You should make yourself more comfortable, don't ya think?

Avery looks confused, then looks down at her clothes.

Dissolve to hallway outside College Classroom. Afternoon. Agent Cavell, phone at his ear, walks slowly down the same hallway the philosophers had previously passed. He carefully opens doors, peering into each classroom.

AGENT CAVELL

(to phone)

No. An anonymous text, actually. Thought maybe Howie was having a little fun with me.

He comes to the classroom in which they had their training exercises. The door is already open. He looks in and flips on the light-switch.

Campus Bushes. Same time. Henri and Guy recline beside their mopeds on a slightly concealed knoll. A pair of venti Starbucks cups rests between them (the names "Tolstoy" and "Franco" are scrawled in marker on the cups). Guy, a set of earphones around his neck, flips through a copy of Maxim magazine. Henri jolts up as the classroom lights come on in the distance. He snaps his fingers to Guy and positions his binoculars for a closer look. Guy awkwardly raises an oversize boom microphone and levels it toward the classroom. He repositions his earphones in an attempt to 'eavesdrop' on the room.

Inside, Cavell walks around the classroom looking for details and holds phone to his ear. Outside, Guy adjusts his volume frequency.

AGENT CAVELL

(to phone)

It's cleared out, Chief.

(beat)

Well, goose-chase does come to mind. Anyway, what's the hold-up on the autopsy?

Enters new room.

No. Yeah, well, I'll drop the items off at the local PD to run some prints. Meantime, want me to look into this medical-research lead outside of town?

He turns toward the desk with the photo of Baptiste on it.

Call you back.

Outside, Henri catches a glimpse of the photo, now held aloft in Agent Cavell's latex gloved-hands. He nudges Guy on the shoulder.

HENRI

(in French)

What is he saying?

Guy lowers one earphone. Shrugs shoulders.

GUY

(in French)

Won't translate.

Henri looks at him in consternation. Guy fiddles with the mic device to replay the sound.

One second.

Inside, Agent Cavell takes a seat in a desk and continues looking at photo. He shakes his head and smiles.

AGENT CAVELL

Sonofabitch.

He sets it down and cradles his hands behind his head. The initials of "Stuart M" stand out to him on the chalkboard. He steps closer to the board.

Sonofabitch.

Outside, Guy hits a button on the recorder and lowers an earphone.

GUY

(thickly accented)

'Medical research.'

Henri lowers his binoculars and locks eyes with Guy. Guy offers him the earphone. Henri gets up quickly and grabs his moped helmet.

¤

Roadside Turnoff near Bare Republic. Late afternoon. Guy and Henri peel their mopeds through the same turnoff Avery and Simeon passed through earlier. The Hearse pulls out of the Bare Republic driveway, nearly colliding with the mopeds. The hookah pipe rattles and Avery and Simeon lurch forward. An open aloe-vera bottle bounds from Avery's hands against the windshield. The mopeds fishtail around them. All parties do alarmed double-takes at each other. Guy and Henri fire their mopeds on down the road past the driveway. Avery catches a slow-motion glimpse of the two, recognizing them. Cranes her head around after them.

AVERY

The hell!?

She turns her sun-burned face to Simeon in alarm. He shrugs his shoulders and fiddles with the stereo while pulling out toward the main road. Avery looks again through the rear of the hearse, then turns her head back to face the road before them. Simeon drops the hookah hardware in her lap.

SIMEON

Mind firing up some apricot?

A police squad car sirens toward then past them on the main road, moving to their right. It is following a pickup truck. Avery cranes her head at the scene, then looks back through the hearse as Simeon turns left.

AVERY

Turn her around!

She hits Simeon's shoulder.

Around man! I think the guy in the truck was a minority.

Simeon obliges with a sweeping U-turn. Gravel sprays off the shoulder. The squad car has the pickup over on the roadside up ahead. Simeon brakes and pulls over, keeping a cautious distance. Guy and Henri covertly brake their mopeds to a distant shoulder and position their video camera toward the scene.

Go check it out.

SIMEON

Huh!? Why me? I'm just—

AVERY

Cause I just spent two hours playing croquet in the feckin' sun, man.

Simeon furrows his brow. Avery pops a pill and nods toward the scene ahead.

I'll man the ride.

Simeon reluctantly unstraps his seat-belt and hauls himself out. He smooths back his hair and begins walking toward the squad car, taking nervous glances back at the hearse. Avery watches in anticipation.

Nearing the scene, Simeon leans forward to try and get a glimpse of the pickup's driver. The POLICE OFFICER turns abruptly. Simeon waves, salutes.

SIMEON

What's the status here officer?

The Officer points a stern finger at him.

POLICE OFFICER

You! Get on the ground!

Simeon cranes his neck forward and sees that the PICKUP DRIVER is a white guy in a tank-top.

SIMEON

Oh, shi—

POLICE OFFICER

On the ground!

Avery watches from the hearse, nervously sucking on a hose and waving away the smoke. In the distance, Guy focuses his camera on the scene. Simeon half-raises both hands.

SIMEON

It's cool, man. A citizen's intervention. It's cool.

POLICE OFFICER

I'm gonna intervene on yer ass if you don't put your face on that gravel right now!

Simeon shakes his head as though the Officer just doesn't get it. As the Officer approaches him, Simeon sees that he is Asian. And, he is a she.

SIMEON

Hey. Hey man, ma'am, madam ladycop, so where you from?

The Officer radios for backup while removing a baton from her belt.

I respect that. I respect that. I mean, here you are trying to enforce a little civic order.

The Officer draws nearer, twirling baton. Simeon sits on his knees, hands behind head.

Hey, maybe we could go for a drink, play a round of Scrabble, talk justice.

The Officer removes a pair of handcuffs from her belt. The pickup suddenly peels away behind her. Simeon turns and runs to the hearse. Avery jumps into the driver's seat and revs the engine. Guy lowers his camera and throws Henri a sly smile.

Dissolve to St. Augustine Police Headquarters. Evening. Agent Cavell sits at a table in the break-room, reading The Republic, *chewing gum. He is constructing a diagram of Plato's Cave Allegory (and many question marks) on a legal pad. A door squeeks open outside. The Baptiste photo and assorted printouts land on Cavell's table. Cavell looks at them then quickly looks up. A local CRIME LAB TECHNICIAN stands before him, crunching an apple.*

CRIME LAB TECHNICIAN

Prints all over it. Multiple subjects. We ran 'em through the international network and turned up some stories. Not exactly watchlist material, but there you go.

Agent Cavell opens up the printout.

AGENT CAVELL

Much obliged. What about the—

CRIME LAB TECHNICIAN

—A pair of print matches on the bottle. Shower cap was clean. No surprise there.

He bites the apple.

AGENT CAVELL

The book?

CRIME LAB TECHNICIAN

Nothing.

AGENT CAVELL

Coffee swabs?

The Technician tosses his apple in a trashcan. Wipes his palms.

CRIME LAB TECHNICIAN

One was a bit off.

Agent Cavell leans back and clasps his hands behind his head.

Looks like someone switched the sugar
with enough Valium to drop a horse.

AGENT CAVELL

Jesus.

CRIME LAB TECHNICIAN

So what's this all about, anyway?

Cavell exhales and turns his gaze to the window.

AGENT CAVELL

Ever study philosophy?

Dissolve to Mother T's Bar. Evening. Avery, Simeon, and Barrett are slouched around a table in the back corner of the bar. Empty VidaStouts abound. Barrett has his arm in a sling. Tommy and KID 1 are at an adjacent table wearing 'Pint-Size Scholar' hats and working on homework. Simeon has KID 1 engaged in a game of Scrabble. An air of futility hangs over the philosophers.

AVERY

You know what our problem is?

Simeon finishes a triumphant Scrabble move against KID 1. Belches.

Bad data.

Counts on her fingers.

We were selective, deliberate, informed,
and then it turns out—

BARRETT

—The people of this fair city know nothing about being oppressed.

He raises an empty glass over his shoulder toward the bar.

Mon, frere!

KID 1

(to Simeon)

Can we work on my spelling test now?

Simeon stares at him incredulously.

SIMEON

Look, sport, Scrabble is your spelling test. Right? The oppression of grammar is like the parakeet in the mineshaft. Dig?

He nods to the board.

I before E except after C. Your move.

Avery pops a pill. Barrett lights a cigarillo.

AVERY

Maybe we need a different methodology.

She picks up a copy of Adbusters *and a pad of post-it notes. Barrett grunts.*

Convenience Store. Late evening. Guy is loading large bags of ice into the trunk of a taxi. A car door shuts nearby. Agent Cavell, phone in hand, heads behind Guy for the store entrance.

AGENT CAVELL

(to phone)

No, a search Howie. The datab—

(beat)

Look, I dunno, kid, the whole deal feels like a circus.

Guy cracks the back of his head on the trunk-door at the sound of Agent Cavell's voice and curses in muffled French. He makes eye contact with Cavell under his shoulder while cowering in pain.

No I know it's delicate, and no I don't really care why.

He opens the door to store.

But what I do care about is motive and
that's where you come in.

The TAXI DRIVER peers under the side of the trunk at Guy, and nods to his head.

TAXI DRIVER

Try some ice on it?

Guy winces, straightens up, and follows Agent Cavell into the store at a cautious distance.

Inside the store, Guy heads for the magazine rack as Agent Cavell pulls a burrito out of the freezer case and loads it in the store microwave.

AGENT CAVELL

(to phone)

No, MacPherson, M-A-C, first name
Stuart. Got it?

Guy listens intently, magazine surreptitiously in hand, head throbbing. Agent Cavell shuts the door of the microwave and turns to the drink display fridge. He beholds a sea of orange Gatorades.

(to phone)

So run it and get me an address.

He pauses and sees in the glass reflection that Guy is watching him.

(to phone)

No, kid, it ain't listed, obviously. And find out what's keeping the damn coroner's office while yer at it.

He shuts the fridge door, hangs up, and pops open the microwave. He subtly raises his eyes in the direction of the magazine rack, but shows no great concern. Guy awkwardly buries himself in a magazine while rubbing his head. Agent Cavell collects his items and walks around the display cases toward the rack and Guy. On the way, he grabs something from the medical section. Guy continues to play it 'cool'.

Agent Cavell stops right beside him. Guy has a gay men's magazine raised in front of his face. Cavell beholds the flamboyant cover, clears his throat, and taps a box of Tylenol on the magazine. Guy, with a look of panic, slowly lowers the magazine and sees Cavell staring at him over the Tylenol.

This might help.

(off magazine)

Careful with that stuff.

Guy awkwardly accepts the Tylenol then looks down at the magazine and a large photo spread of two men getting intimate. He reddens and looks at Cavell. Cavell smiles and turns to the magazine rack. He makes a quick scan and picks up a copy of Foreign Affairs. *He gives Guy a pat on the back and heads for the counter. Guy hastily switches magazines.*

Agent Cavell pays then heads for the door. Guy, now with National Geographic *in hand, nods toward Cavell and shakes the Tylenol.*

GUY

Merci.

Cavell nods with a light smile and exits. Shakes his head.

Inside Mother T's Bar. Late evening. A door jingles. Stuart, a large white-board in tow, struggles to haul himself through the bar entrance. He nods a smile to the bartender, DALE, who comes to relieve him of the whiteboard. Tommy is seated on the counter, throwing darts.

STUART

Thought we'd diagram some sentences this time. Or at least go through the motions. Whaddaya think? Could always de-diagram 'em too.

Dale gives a thumbs-up and sets up the board in front of the counter and an oversize sign for VidaStout Microbrews. Stuart gives Tommy a high-five, glimpses the philosophers in the back and nods a smile. He dumps his bag and camera on the counter beside a large cardboard package.

DALE

Just in from Elmo. Fed-exed the damn thing.

He steps around the back of the bar and starts pulling Stuart a draught.

STUART

Huh.

He cuts open the top and pulls out a handful of colorful brochures. Kindly accepts the drink from Dale.

No shit! Man, he really is hot about this.

Dale takes a gander. The brochure is adorned with a photo of a group of happy school-kids standing outside Mother T's. Dale reads the title.

DALE

'The VidaStout Community: Taking Pint-Size Global.'

He looks to Stuart.

You know about this?

Stuart shakes his head.

STUART

I mean, he said something about a new marketing venture, but—

Avery approaches the counter looking haggard.

Ave! Hey, take a look at this.

He shoves a brochure in front of her.

AVERY

Hey man. So listen, you got an office around here? Thought I might run some internet searches. . . Cute. A little bizarre, but—

A phone rings behind the counter. Dale shoulders a beer towel and grabs it.

Anyway, office?

DALE

(to phone)

Sure thing Mr. Exum, just walked in. By the way, how's the liver holding up? Hang on a sec.

He hands the cordless phone across the counter to Stuart. Chattering issues from the phone. Stuart points Avery to a doorway off the back of the room. He throws a quick drinking motion toward Barrett and Simeon, then points Dale to the tap for a few more draughts.

STUART

(to phone)

No, yeah, they look great!

(beat)

Say again?

He lodges the phone against his shoulder and takes the serving tray of drinks and heads toward the back table to join Barrett and Simeon. Simeon has corralled Kid 1 and KID 2 into a game of cutthroat Hangman on a menu chalkboard.

SIMEON

Hey! First noose, then head. Don't be messin with me man.

(beat)

Q.

Stuart rests the tray on the table and nods to Barrett and Simeon. Barrett grunts and rubs his hands together. Stuart drops a couple of menus on the table. Simeon harnesses his beer.

R.

STUART

(to phone; worked up)

No, I get it. It's just—

(beat)

Right! Like the One campaign or that Red iPod thing.

He slides Barrett and Simeon a couple of the brochures.

I just didn't expect, you know, well, such a big step. Paris, I mean, hey. But, no, right, it's genius Mr. Exum.

(beat)

Yessir. Yessir I got a passport somewhere. Wow. Okay.

Barrett leafs through the brochure.

Yes, I feel you sir.

Simeon, with one eye on the Hangman board, cocks a curious eyebrow.

VidaStout never bluffs, sir.

(beat)

Will do. And good luck with the transplant, sir.

He clicks off and shakes his head in a disbelieving smile. To Barrett/Simeon,

Wow. Sorry. My boss is sort of a visionary.

He nods to the brochures as a case in point.

(to KIDS)

Hey Jordan, Molly! Ya'll want some juice?

Simeon loses his round of Hangman and chucks an eraser at the board.

BARRETT

Ahh, times are hard.

Stuart nods dumbly, reaches for a drink. A thought occurs to him and he tilts his head toward the office entrance.

STUART

So what's up? How's the activism?

Barrett finishes his drink, dabs his forehead with a handkerchief. Simeon studies the menu.

BARRETT

Seems history doesn't favor us. Might have to market our services elsewhere.

SIMEON

This on the house, right?

STUART

Oh yeah, yeah, course.

Silent beat. Stuart takes a drink and fiddles with a VidaStout coaster. Then drops the coaster in a sudden jolt.

Hey, you guys ever think about corporate sponsorship? Seed capital?

Simeon studies the menu. Barrett blows his nose.

SIMEON

I only work on Leibniz.

Confused beat.

STUART

No. No I don't mean philosophically. I mean, well, sponsors, you know. Capital.

Barrett locks eyes with Stuart. Simeon looks up at Barrett. Stuart looks at them both. They all look down at the brochures.

Dissolve to Convention Center Exercise Facility. Simone is on a massage table getting worked over by a HOTEL ATTENDANT. Steam clouds the air. Henri is seated on a nearby counter, sweating profusely through his black mock-turtleneck and chugging a 2-liter of Diet Coke. He snaps his cell-phone shut, exhales, and towels off his face. Simone moans pleasurably as the masseuse works her shoulders. Doesn't break her trance.

HENRI

(accented English)

So, he's not on our trail.

SIMONE

And Barrett's party?

Henri smirks and hands Simone a bottled water (Elan Vital).

HENRI

More useful than expected.

Simone unscrews the cap and motions for a paper cup.

SIMONE

Good. What about our fundraising?
Global affiliates?

Henri nods and reaches for a cup for Simone.

HENRI

Supply and demand, you know.

Swigs his drink. Simone rolls over to receive a mud-mask.

SIMONE

The right hand need not know the work
of the left.

Henri swigs, eyes his left hand, swishes, and nods.

I'm to return to Paris tomorrow following the closing ceremony here. Perhaps there is a public appearance I can use to leverage the international momentum.

Henri stands with the towel around his neck and hands the masseuse a $10, and the rest of his Diet Coke.

You and Guy will oversee the clinic work on this end. But don't lose track of the Americans. Sometimes even the smallest fly can turn the horse, you understand.

Henri nods and blows his nose in the towel.

I want to know who's backing them. If they so much as wash dishes in a soup kitchen I want to know about it.

HENRI

God forbid.

SIMONE

Precisely.

Dissolve to Mother T's Bar. Inside Stuart's office. Night. A weary Avery sits before a desktop computer running Internet searches on the Google page.

AVERY

'Oppression' comma 'human bondage.'

She hits the 'Enter' key and waits.

Whoa.

Squints at screen.

Not that kind of bondage.

She takes a deep breath and starts typing a new search.

'Injustice' comma 'ethics' comma 'advocacy.'

Hits 'Enter.' Squints at screen. Reads:

'American philosophers on the loose.'

(beat)

The hell?

A YouTube clip begins to play, rolling footage of Simeon's altercation with the Cop, Tanya running mad through the streets, a topless Avery playing croquet, and Barrett running from the warehouse Foreman.

As Avery sits stunned, Stuart enters the room behind her, tosses phone on couch, and stands with his hands on his hips. Avery's eyes are transfixed on the monitor.

STUART

Okay. This is gonna sound—

AVERY

—Fuck me.

STUART

—crazy. Huh?

Avery slams the mouse against the monitor.

AVERY

We're on the net, man! We're on the goddam world wide feckin web!

Stuart leans over her shoulder as the clip replays. Avery drops her head in her hands. On the clip Barrett is hauling ass.

STUART

Man, the old guy can really move. You got a film crew?

Avery looks up at the screen, her hands still plated against her face.

AVERY

Shit. Shit. Shit, Stu.

Stuart checks the clip details.

STUART

Uploaded by, hang on, 'maximman'. Huh. So—

AVERY

Shit, Stu! Not good, man. Not good. Do you realize how fast this link will spread through every philosophy department, hiring committee, graduate blog . . . Shit!

Stuart straightens up. Gestures to the monitor.

STUART

So, you mean—

Convention Center Lecture Hall. Same time. Conference-goers mingle about with drinks and popcorn as the YouTube clip plays (to their great shock and delight) on the oversize screen behind the podium. Simone, standing in the back of the room, smiles and shrugs her shoulders to a passerby. As the clip concludes a viewer hoists his popcorn.

Mother T's Bar. Office. Same time. Avery's face is buried in her hands. Stuart walks back to the couch, picks up a handful of darts, and sits down.

STUART

There is some good news.

Avery throws her head back on the chair. Stuart puts on a Pint-Size Scholars cap. Tosses another one on the desk beside the monitor.

Pint-Size is going international and you guys are consultants. Elmo ate it up! We're on a plane tomorrow.

Avery swivels her chair to look at him. Stuart straightens his cap and flips a dart.

AVERY

(nonplussed)

Some dumbass with a camera just flushed my career and you're telling me I have a future as a goodwill ambassador for a beer company, and this is good news?

She turns her chair back to face the monitor. Stuart straightens up to reclaim the moment.

STUART

Hey. It's what you wanted, right? Justice and all that?

He hands her one of the brochures, taps it.

Look. So maybe what you're looking for is in Europe, you know? Hell maybe Asia? Anyway, no one could say you didn't have the balls to try the unexpected.

Avery scans her latest Google results.

AVERY

Three-thousand-plus hits. Minus our own. And can we please leave the 'balls' out of it.

STUART

Ave.

He swivels her chair to face him.

Look, forget the conference. Forget everything. What about Baptiste? 'Find the least of these', right?

She looks at him, weighing the situation.

AVERY

That's idealism, Stu.

Counts on her fingers.

Aristotle's 'mean', Kant's 'categorical imperative', Mill's 'competent judge', Levinas' 'other'. Ideals, man.

Stuart eyes her intently.

STUART

Whoa, hey. Look, Ave, I knew you when idealism was the only thing worth having.

She looks at him. She sniffles back some stress tears, softens.

AVERY

So this Elmo, whoever he is, he's not going to F us over, right?

Stuart shakes his head.

I wanna do some good, Stu.

She wipes her nose with Elmo's embroidered handkerchief.

Some good.

(to self)

But what is good?

Stuart nods, gives a quizzical look at the handkerchief.

STUART

You will. I'll cover the logistics for Paris, then Asia. Hopefully run some wire reports to cover the PR and stuff, so—

She raises her hands at the monitor.

AVERY

Paris!? Asia!? We need some leads, man. Leads.

Stuart aims a dart.

Shit, Stu!

Gestures to computer. Stuart grabs a brick of office paper from a bookshelf and tosses it to her. He nods to a printer and smiles. Avery stares at him in disbelief. He tosses her another brick of paper.

¤

Cheap Motel Room. Agent Cavell's phone sits atop his copies of the Republic *and* Foreign Affairs. *It rings to the tune of "Bringing Sexy Back." Agent Cavell emerges from the bathroom in a towel and drying his hair. He shakes his head and grimaces at the ring-tone.*

AGENT CAVELL

Jesus, Howie.

Dissolve to Mother T's Bar. Outside. Morning. A 'Paradise Franks' hot-dog vendor wheels by. Simeon, cup of coffee in hand, hauls luggage into the back of his hearse. Avery and Stuart come out of the bar, step past a sleeping Homeless Man, and file into the hearse where Barrett is already seated, dozing, wearing a Pint-Size cap. Stuart moves Barrett's legs to make room. He holds two office-paper boxes of printouts on his lap.

Simeon starts the engine with a plume of smoke just as Agent Cavell rounds the corner in his rental car. Guy and Henri shoot through an alleyway en route to the bar. Cavell pulls to the curb and steps out. Guy and Henri brake a short distance away and look with surprise at Cavell, then the Hearse. They screech their mopeds around Cavell's car in pursuit of the hearse. Cavell turns in confused alarm but doesn't put it together. He checks the address and steps over the Homeless Man to enter Mother T's.

Revving the Hearse through a yellow light, Simeon turns on some music and hands Avery a spoon and lighter for the hookah pipe.

AVERY

Ain't it a bit early, man?

Stuart, looking through the back of the vehicle, sees the mopeds coming on.

STUART

Hey we got company.

Simeon checks his mirrors.

SIMEON

God. Those crotch-rockets are soo retro-nihilist.

(beat)

You want a piece!?

(to Avery)

Hang on.

He pulls on the emergency brake and executes a sharp turn. Stuart plants an arm against the roof for support. Barrett dozes.

Used to do funerals in college.

The mopeds zip back into view.

Oh, you want some more?

Inside Mother T's Bar. Same time. Agent Cavell stands at the bar leaning over a photo of a disheveled Stuart. Dale stands across the counter from him. Dated mug shots of Avery, Simeon, and Barrett are also laid out. Dale smiles at Stuart's shot.

DALE

Oh man. I do remember that night. St. Paddy's. Hoo-eeh.

AGENT CAVELL

So, Stuart Macpherson?

DALE

One and only.

AGENT CAVELL

He a philosopher?

Dale shelves some pint glasses.

DALE

He's just about everything. A one-man revolution.

(beat)

You one of Elmo's partners?

Hearse. St. Augustine Streets. Same time. Simeon executes another sharp turn. He nearly misses the very same Officer he encountered days before. Offers her a mock salute on the fly. The mopeds careen through the turn, but are cut off by the squad car. Simeon floors the hearse down an alley, bangs through a garbage can, jumps a curb, and screeches into the cover of a car wash bay.

As sirens fade outside, the team breathes a collective sigh of relief. Much to their surprise, three rather buxom, and near-topless BABES surround the hearse with oversize sponges and a playful spray of water. Their scant T-shirts read "Buff n'Buff." Barrett awakes. His eyes blink then focus upward on BABE 1's breasts outside his window. Clears his throat.

BARRETT

I dare say she's not the least of these.

Stuart waves awkwardly to BABE 2 through the back window.

Dissolve to St. Augustine airport runway/hanger. Day. A private jet, the 'VidaStout' logo shining bright in the sun, stands parked outside a hanger. MECHANICS pull a fuel hose away from its tank.

The Hearse cruises in and parks at an angle beside the jet. All four doors open simultaneously and the team members step out. They pause to admire the plane. A support crew loads several large crates of VidaStout beer. Simeon pops the back doors open. The luggage bay on the plane opens.

Slow motion. They march in a single file line with their luggage toward the jet. Stuart leads and nods to the pilot. Barrett and Simeon follow. Avery pauses, takes a deep breath with her head toward the sky, then marches on.

Top of Parking Garage. Same time. Henri and Guy park their mopeds and pull off their helmets. They look around the streets below, then at each other. Guy shrugs his shoulders. Henri looks skyward and sees a jet rising toward the clouds. Guy follows his gaze, then takes a bite of a Snickers Bar.

Outside Mother T's Bar. Same time. Agent Cavell bounds out of the entrance as Tommy and Kid 2 slap low-fives to the Homeless Man on their way in.

Cavell, a Vida Stout brochure in hand, races down the sidewalk toward his car. Hears the low-flying jet overhead. Comes to a panting halt. Looks up. Clasps his hands behind his head. The same jet climbs skyward.

Convention Center Lecture Hall. Same time. Simone, wearing the SPEK Medal, stands contentedly before the audience of philosophers. Applause. Behind her on the large screen is a Powerpoint image of an emaciated child, and this overlaid with the following text:

"A New Era of Academic Activism."

¤

French Countryside. Day. A sightseeing bus creeps up a winding road as an airplane passes overhead. The reflection of the airplane passes over Avery's sunglasses as she cranes her head against the bus window. She fans herself with a handful of Google printouts. Simeon plies his instructive craft on Stuart, the captive audience.

SIMEON

No. You're missing the point. I'm not saying Patrick Swayze is a communist.

Barrett is sleeping against Avery's shoulder with a handkerchief matted against his forehead. The bus is crammed with luggage and tourists, all in the sweltering heat of a Paris summer. Avery studies her printouts, marking certain items with a Sharpie.

I'm simply suggesting that the whole leit motif of *Red Dawn* is a subversion of capitalist-democracy, possibly even unbeknownst to the cast.

Simeon and Stuart are crammed in a nearby row of seats with an ASIAN GIRL reading a Hunger Games *book between them. Simeon, sweating through a "Just Preach It" T-shirt, chows on a crepe and pulls on a VidaStout through a straw. Stuart, his eyes drifting out the bus windows, swigs a bottle of water.*

STUART

But they all die, right. For the most part.

SIMEON

(mouthful)

Most die. A few live on to establish a race of equals.

(beat)

If one may surmise.

The bus brakes sharply and Simeon leans into the Asian Girl. Notices her book.

No shit. Is that the fourth installment?

Avery and Stuart look intently out the windows. They catch each other's eyes and nod. Avery gives Barrett a gentle elbow. The bus enters a historic town district and heaves its way down Boulevard Henry IV.

Bastille 'entrance.' Day. Stuart, Simeon, Avery, and a yawning Barrett step from the bus and stand together to take in the sight. The Bastille remains rest before them beyond an iron fence, somewhat smaller than history.

SIMEON

Huh. When did they move it underground?

The sound of children chanting drifts their way.

FRENCH SCHOOLCHILDREN

(singing)

La tour Eiffel a quatre pieds; Il en faut deux pour y monter, Et pour s'aider, on peut chanter,

A,B,C,D . . .

Stuart taps Avery and nods. A crowd of CHILDREN are grouped together nearby. A flamboyant PHOTOGRAPHER cranks his tripod and gestures to them to close ranks. Avery cradles her stack of papers against her chest. Barrett lights a cigarillo and shields his eyes from the sun.

AVERY

Is that us?

STUART

That's us.

SIMEON

Monument? I could fit this sucker in my carry-on.

The Photographer waves excitedly to them. Stuart returns a wave. Photographer yells.

PHOTOGRAPHER

(accented English)

VidaStout delegation, no?!

Stuart bows. The Photographer pumps his fist.

Right on time. The light is splendid!

He waves them over. The children wave and yell to them. Avery, Barrett, Stuart, and Simeon stand uncomfortably amid the chaos of schoolchildren, the Bastille stones in the background. A CHAPERONE passes out placards blazened with the VidaStout logo. The Photographer desperately tries to direct the group and motions for happy faces. Avery tucks her paperwork under her arm and obliges the photographer by wrapping an arm around a nearby schoolgirl.

The Photographer stops and turns about to grab a large rolled-up banner. He presents this to the Chaperone and points her to the group. The Chaperone approaches the group and unfurls the banner for the front row (philosophers included) to hold. The banner makes its way through the chaos of hands. It reads:

Pint-Size Scholars, Europe: Education Breaks Chains!

The Photographer approaches the Chaperone with a long oversize chain and directs her to have the group hoist this up alongside the banner.

AVERY

My God, Elmo. Spare no drama.

The chain makes its way across the front row as the Photographer positions his camera. A black sedan pulls up to the curb. A smartly dressed FEMALE ASSISTANT steps out of the driver's side and steps over to the passenger side to open the door. Simone emerges in a black suit and sunglasses. She runs a brush through her hair and hands the brush to her Assistant. The cigarillo drops from Barrett's mouth. Avery's jaw drops. Stuart kids with one of the children.

Stu?

STUART

Uh-huh.

AVERY

Mind telling me what—

Stuart looks up.

STUART

Hey, isn't that the—

BARRETT

Princess of the Parisian Reds.

Simeon takes notice.

SIMEON

Enchanté

STUART

What the hell is—

As the philosophers stand in collective awe, Simone butters up the Photographer with pleasantries and smiles. The Assistant eyes the philosophers with suspicion. The Photographer gestures for her to join the photo. Simone hands the Assistant her purse and marches over to the group. She attempts to squeeze her way into the front row next to Avery and Barrett.

SIMONE

(in accented English)

Barrett, darling.

BARRETT

Lady Marseilles.

SIMONE

A touch out of your element don't you think?

Barrett fumbles for words and drops his share of the banner/chain. Stuart nods hello to Simone and forces a smile. Simeon throws a sweaty hand Simone's way.

SIMEON

I'm Simeon. Leibniz studies.

(beat)

My you have exquisite skin.

Simone smiles. Avery rolls her eyes in disgust.

AVERY

(to Simone, bitterly)

So. What brings you to the Bastille on Bastille Day, Dr. Marseilles?

(beat)

Fascist rally later?

Simone plays it cool and lovingly pats a child's head. The Photographer yells for everyone's attention and motions for the group to bunch up more tightly. Simone wraps her hands around the banner and chain.

SIMONE

The Education Ministry asked me to come and lend credibility to this interesting spectacle. Naturally I—

Avery tugs on the chain.

AVERY

—hardly expected to find us?

Simone tugs back.

SIMONE

A charming surprise.

(to Barrett)

Seems we've found a way to work together again, mon cher.

The Photographer yells desperately as the children impatiently break ranks. Barrett struggles for words. Avery and Simone continue tugging the chain.

SIMEON

Hey could somebody fill me in here?

AVERY

(sternly)

Whatever your angle is, scholar, this is our deal so—

A resolved tug from Simone.

SIMONE

—Promoting underprivileged education
falls within the purview of—

Barrett mouths a fresh cigarillo then looks down in alarm as smoke rises from his pant-cuffs.

BARRETT

(shrieks)

I'm on fire! Fire!

He shakes his lost cigarillo from a pant-cuff and stomps about madly. An all-out tug-of-war over the chain ensues. Avery's Google printouts scatter in the wind.

SIMEON

There goes Europe.

Children scream and beat the philosophers with their placards. Simone shrieks and heaves on the chain. The Photographer throws up his hands, curses, then snaps a photo.

¤

Paris Police Station. A camera flashes on Avery, Stuart, Barrett, and Simeon as they stand against a lineup wall.

Stuart is holding a VidaStout placard. Barrett's ankle is wrapped in gauze.

Agent Cavell stands behind the glass observation wall with a FRENCH POLICE DETECTIVE. He rubs his hand across his tired face, spits his gum into a nearby trashcan, and accepts a cup of coffee from the Detective.

AGENT CAVELL

Yup, those are ours.

The philosophers turn to exit the lineup area. Simeon smells his armpit. The Detective frowns and presses a folded newspaper against Agent Cavell's chest. Cavell sets his coffee down and opens the paper.

White Limousine. Day. Elmo Exum, seated in a white 1980s cruising limo, opens up a newspaper and scratches his dog (CAESAR). His eyes widen. On the front page of the International section is a photo of the philosophers caught in pandemonium with Simone over the VidaStout banner and chain.

ELMO EXUM

My stars, boy!

Caesar whimpers pitifully. Elmo, beet red, puts on his reading glasses and studies the article. Reads:

'A group of American scholars visiting France on behalf of an American microbrew good-will effort reportedly assualted—'

Paris Police Station. Interrogation Room. Avery sits on a table, newspaper in hand. Reads:

AVERY

—a French intellectual outside the Bastille. Mlle Simone Marseilles stated that the American philosophers were a rogue band of capitalist rebels attempting to incite widespread revolt under the guise of social and political ethics.'

She slams the paper on the table.

SIMEON

Pretty much.

Stuart leans over the newspaper. Reads:

STUART

'None of the Americans were available for comment.'

Barrett props his leg on the table and winces.

BARRETT

Nor the Brit, as it were.

Avery stands and covers her face with her hands.

AVERY

Un-feckin-believable.

She reaches in her pocket for her pill case. She tries the other pocket.

STUART

Not exactly the press Elmo was gunning for.

AVERY

Where are my pills?

(beat)

My pills, people! *People*, my pills!

She turns to the door and yanks it open, nearly colliding with Agent Cavell. They face each other for an awkward moment. Cavell holds his briefcase and cup of coffee. He motions as if to enter.

AGENT CAVELL

Mind if I?

Avery steps aside.

Thank you.

The door swings shut. Agent Cavell places his briefcase on the table.

Take your seats please.

They gather around the table. The newspaper remains on the table's center.

SIMEON

(sotto to Stuart)

He with Elmo?

Stuart shrugs his shoulders. Agent Cavell lays his badge on the table and clears his throat.

AGENT CAVELL

I'm Agent James Cavell, United States Homeland Security.

Digs in his briefcase.

I handle the liaison work abroad, case you're wondering. There's been a lot of restructuring.

He tosses his copy of The Republic *onto the newspaper and peels a stick of gum into his mouth. Quoting,*

'He lives along day by day.'

Simeon leans in for a look.

SIMEON

No shit! Is that the Bloom translation!?

BARRETT

Holy mother.

AGENT CAVELL

Socrates. Book Eight. 'Gratifying the desires that occur to him. At one time drinking and listening to the flute, at another,' well, 'spending his time as though he were occupied with philosophy.'

Simeon closes his eyes in reflection. Barrett mouths the ancient words.

'Often he engages in politics and, jumping up, says and does—'

AVERY

(arms crossed, nodding)

'—whatever chances to come to him.'

AGENT CAVELL

So. That's one man's republic.

He pulls a stack of file folders from his briefcase and drops them on the table.

And that's ours. Meaning you.

The philosophers look at one another nervously.

Now, for starters, the locals have revoked your tourist privileges. I'll take that as assumed.

STUART

So—

AGENT CAVELL

So why am I wasting my time gladhanding French authorities to drag your butts back to Washington?

AVERY

I'm sorry. Is it a crime to be—

AGENT CAVELL

Philosophers? No. But when a bunch of intellectuals start acting like Geraldo and rough up a local dignitary, it gets complicated.

He turns to his files.

SIMEON

I thought our transcripts were sealed.

Avery tugs the newspaper from underneath the stack and holds their photo aloft. She slaps Simone's image.

AVERY

Dignitary!? I'm sorry, man, but this is a set up.

Agent Cavell looks at her, looks at Stuart, then turns his attention to the folders.

Outside. Simone's car pulls up. She exits out the passenger side and saunters toward the entrance, a newspaper under her arm.

Inside Interrogation Room. Agent Cavell opens the top file on his stack.

AGENT CAVELL

Let's see, Barrett—

Avery groans over her stomach.

AVERY

Aagh! I don't believe this.

BARRETT

(to Agent Cavell)

—You should be aware I have tenure.

AGENT CAVELL

(reads)

Age 51. Trespassing on royal hunting grounds.

BARRETT

I was lost.

AGENT CAVELL

(continuing)

In a guerrilla costume.

BARRETT

Very lost.

Agent Cavell moves on to the next file.

AGENT CAVELL

Stuart MacPherson. Driving under the influence.

STUART

Sure sure. It was St. Paddy's day, man. I mean—

AGENT CAVELL

Any other influences Mr. MacPherson, like, say, I dunno, Marx?

STUART

(confused)

Groucho?

Agent Cavell gives him a stern look then opens the next file.

AGENT CAVELL

Avery Meir—

Avery raises her hand.

AVERY

Present your honor.

AGENT CAVELL

Alleged indecent exposure at one 'Banana Republic.' Charges pending.

BARRETT

(gasps)

I won't believe it!

SIMEON

You shop at the outlets?

AVERY

Bare Republic.

AGENT CAVELL

Right.

(skimming)

Defendant failed to make court appearance.

Avery shakes her head. Agent Cavell moves on.

Simeon Napp. Discharging a firearm in a public library.

Silence.

SIMEON

The Critical Theory section needed some culling.

Agent Cavell closes the file.

AGENT CAVELL

I think the Friends of the Library disagreed.

(beat, to all)

So. You mind telling me what you're up to?

Silence. Avery reaches for the Republic *and flips through it.*

Station Entrance. Simone steps through a doorway and greets the Police Detective with a customary kiss on the cheek. She turns to behold the viewing window and the spectacle of her rivals being interrogated. Her face fills with sweet satisfaction. The Detective pours her a cup of coffee. Cheers.

Inside Interrogation Room. Agent Cavell pushes back from the table and clasps his hands behind his head.

AGENT CAVELL

C'mon. We've been getting phone calls.

He pulls the Baptiste photo from his briefcase and lays it on the table.

This gentleman takes a fall and you people are all over the scene.

He slides the photo of Baptiste with the guerrilla fighter alongside the first photo. Simone strains her neck before the glass to get a bead on the curious photo.

AGENT CAVELL

What is it? Violence? Envy? Idealism? Boredom? I'm just trying to connect some dots here.

AVERY

(pleading)

It's about justice. Baptiste—

AGENT CAVELL

Now we're talking my language. And Plato's. Of course, by the end of the dialogue—

AVERY

(flatly)

Social justice.

Cavell hefts The Republic.

AGENT CAVELL

Harmony of the parts, no?

AVERY

No. Harmony of THE part. The one in the shadows. In the cold. In the suffering margins of—

She gives out, then takes a curious look at the second photo of Baptiste. Simone follow's Avery's gaze and squints in a second attempt at the photo. Cavell looks to Avery, then the others.

AGENT CAVELL

But, why Europe? Why Simone Marseilles? Why you? If you guys wanted to do some charity work just go join—

AVERY

It's complicated.

AGENT CAVELL

Like I said.

He nods to the first Baptiste photo.

And I don't need to tell you whose fingerprints are all over it.

STUART

Look sir. Alright. Speaking as an unofficial member of the affiliated press corps, seriously, this whole deal is just—

Simone smiles behind the glass.

SIMONE

(to herself)

—too good to be true.

AVERY

—It'll all make sense when we find the Least of These.

Agent Cavell holds eye contact with her. Stuart and Barrett exchange a surprised glance. Behind the glass Simone's eyes widen in alarm. She squeezes her cup.

AGENT CAVELL

Whatever that means, I've got a plane heading back to DC in three hours.

(beat)

We'll have plenty of time to talk philosophy.

Avery grimaces. Silence. She clutches her stomach and leans forward in pain, covertly pinning the second photo of Baptiste under her sleeve.

BARRETT

Are we in Economy or Business Class? Don't say Economy.

Simone turns to the Detective.

SIMONE

(in French, subtitled)

I'll accompany the American officer, if you don't mind.

The Detective pounds the last of his coffee, grunts approvingly, and tosses his cup in a trashcan.

¤

White Limousine. Elmo Exum stands with the help of his cane a few paces from his limo on the shoulder of the dusty side-road not far from the Bare Republic. He struggles to take a leak. His dog does the same nearby. His CHAUFFEUR leans against the hood of the limo smoking a cigarette and reading a map. Elmo has a string of Rosary beads clenched in his teeth. He repositions his cell-phone earpiece and pees into the brush.

ELMO EXUM

(to phone, flustered)

Yes boys, 'course I read the papers. And what I'm telling you is the logic of the new economy flies on publicity. Good, bad, it don't matter.

He winces in discomfort.

If you wanna sell a hog you don't go scrubbing it up and such. You let it stink so's the buyer knows it's active. You follow?

Caesar finishes peeing.

Atta boy, Caesar.

(to phone)

You just gotta sit tight, now. Guerrilla marketing's gonna put us on the map.

He finishes peeing and buckles his trousers.

Whatdya think the good people of European nations are asking themselves right now? I'll tell ya: "Well now, what about this VidaStout beverage?"

Turns back toward limo.

Oh hell no.

(beat)

Got a bum liver, that's how come. Fixin to get me a transplantation from a little outfit down here hither and yon about Saint Auggie's way. Anyhow, my people will deliver the international base, I can assure you that.

(beat)

Okay then.

He pulls out the earpiece and tosses it to his Chauffeur.

CHAUFFEUR

Smooth things over?

Elmo shakes his head and wiggles a finger in his ear. The Chauffeur opens a limo door for Elmo.

ELMO EXUM

If Brother Mac don't get it together we're
gonna be up a creek I shudder to name.

He thumps the inside of the limo's roof with his cane. To dog,

Buckle up, Caesar.

¤

Paris Streets. Police Van. Day. Stuart is seated in the front bench of a van staring at the front and back of the photo of Baptiste with the guerrilla fighter. Avery clutches her stomach and rocks uneasily next to him. Barrett is in the passenger seat, Simeon laid out on the bench behind Stuart and Avery. A disheartened air hangs over the ride. A FRENCH DRIVER turns through loud radio stations.

STUART

(off photo, to Avery)

Doesn't have a name. Just says "ST." I dunno, Ave.

Barrett digs through Avery's purse.

BARRETT

Good grief woman. Where hideth the smokables?

Simeon observes an unmarked police vehicle trailing not far behind the van.

SIMEON

Maybe it means 'saint'.

He squints back at the car.

Inside French Squad Car. Same time. A POLICE DRIVER adjusts his radio. Agent Cavell and Simone are in the back seat. Simone is looking 'admiringly' at the photo of Baptiste from Agent Cavell's file.

AGENT CAVELL

Well, I just hope we can all move on. You'll receive an official letter of apology from the State Department.

Simone smiles and brushes her hair back.

SIMONE

Unnecessary, of course.

She hands the photo back to Agent Cavell.

Were there any others?

Agent Cavell rustles through his file.

AGENT CAVELL

Oh, sure, there was this, ah—

(perplexed)

Hmm.

SIMONE

Hmm?

AGENT CAVELL

I'm sorry, I, ah, seem to have—

Police Van. Same time. Stuart looks again at the photo. Barrett pulls a can of pepper spray out of Avery's purse and looks at it. The van jolts forward through a yellow light.

Squad Car. Cavell's French Driver curses and bangs the steering wheel as the van pulls away from them. He reaches for his radio. Agent Cavell and Simone look at each other.

Van. Avery groans at the jolt of their own vehicle and places a bracing hand on Stuart's shoulder. Stuart lowers the photo and turns to her. Avery groans again, this time with a touch of panic.

SIMEON

Uh-oh.

Avery lurches and sends a spray of vomit across the windshield. The Driver yells in disgust and pounds the steering column. Barrett looks in alarm at the vomit, considers it, then turns to observe the location of Agent Cavell's vehicle.

Whoa.

Barrett makes eye contact with Stuart and Simeon, then nods toward the outside. He pretends to dig through Avery's purse again.

BARRETT

Very well. I've just the thing for motion sickness.

He points the pepper spray at their Driver and unleashes a stinging spray on his face. The Driver shrieks. Barrett reaches over him to unhinge the door.

A thousand apologies, *mon frere.*
Advantage to the greater good.

He opens the Driver's door and kicks him out onto the curb.

There we are. Some air should do.

He slams the door closed, locks it, and nods to Simeon. Simeon barrels forward and jumps into the driver's seat. He floors the van.

Agent Cavell and Simone jump out of their vehicle in helpless alarm. Cavell tries to hail a cab, but chaos reigns and horns blare. Simone shades her eyes with the newspaper and watches the van flee the scene. Across the way, the former van Driver spins madly about the street in his pepper-sprayed blindness. The Driver of the squad car slams his radio in frustration and peels out in hopeless pursuit of the van.

Van. Same time. Stuart cradles Avery's head in his lap. Simeon guns the van through a tight turn and lovingly pats the dash.

SIMEON

C'mon you old sofa-bed.

Stuart wipes Avery's forehead with his sleeve. Avery blinks groggily up at him.

AVERY

Get the Asia list, Stu. The Google.

STUART

Easy now. Easy.

Paris Streets. PEDESTRIANS attempt to calm the frantic van driver down. Agent Cavell surveys the scene, then casts a glance Simone's way. Simone hands him the newspaper and gestures toward the van driver in his hysteria.

SIMONE

I guess you better see to latest victim.

Nodding down the block.

My office is not far. I'll see if I can send in some help.

Agent Cavell nods as she makes her abrupt exit. He turns to cross the street and mend the situation.

Van. Stuart leans his ear over Avery's lips. Her eyes are fluttering.

AVERY

(sotto)

Injustice, Asia. No, Burma.

(beat)

Page 141. Saw it at the station. One-forty—

She passes out. Stuart looks at her in confusion. He reaches across their seat and draws the pile of Google printouts to himself.

Paris Streets. Agent Cavell finishes hoisting the van driver into a cab as the poor soul continues shouting a stream of American-oriented obscenities. Cavell, newspaper still in hand, bangs on the roof of the cab to send it off. He wipes a sleeve across his brow, exhales, turns about wondering which way to go.

Van. Simeon jacks up the radio volume and fists the roof. Barrett whoops loudly and fires a stream of pepper spray out the window as the van bounds onto an expressway. Stuart smiles and looks over his printouts at Avery.

¤

Paris Office Building Entrance. Day. Agent Cavell pushes through the doors and stops before a building legend. He punches his cell-phone and scans the office names as the call crosses the Atlantic.

AGENT CAVELL

(to phone)

Okay kid, I want you to stop whatever it is you're doing and listen real close.

(beat)

No, I don't have a sheath for the sword. Just, no, look—

(beat)

Listen up, alright. I want you to start checking the passenger manifestos on all departing flights from Paris. Standbys especially.

(beat)

I'm aware I have a seat already. No, for the Americans. The philosophers. Okay?

(beat)

And quit messing with my ringtones. You know I can't work this thing.

He shuts the phone and revisits the legend, muttering the titles to himself. He stops on a nondescript title: "Justice Partners" (in French). He mutters the phrase then runs his finger along the line, stopping on "S. Marseilles, PhD." He sees it is listed on the top floor.

A JANITOR brooms the floor in front of him. Cavell races toward the ding of an elevator, and steps in. As the doors begin to close the Janitor's broom jousts its way in and the doors reopen. Cavell, frustrated, makes room for him, then opens his newspaper to the Bastille photo and all its pandemonium. He studies it, and mutters through the opening of the story. The Janitor watches him, then nods to the paper.

JANITOR

Simone Marseilles, c'est ca?

Agent Cavell nods awkwardly. The Janitor taps the photo and smiles.

Simone Marseilles,

ahhh . . .

And tries out his English.

No shit, eh!

Agent Cavell looks up, confused, then shakes his head and nods.

AGENT CAVELL

No shit.

The elevator brakes and the doors slide open. Agent Cavell focuses hard on the paper. He whips out a pen and circles Simone's initials. The Janitor gestures toward the open doors. Cavell is lost in the moment's revelation.

No shit.

He punches the doors closed and turns to the confused Janitor.

Philosophe provocateur, eh?

His cell rings to Howie's "Sexy Back" ringtone. He shuts it off. The Janitor spits in the elevator's corner.

ACT III

"It is a very bad objection to a
philosopher to say that he is
incomprehensible."

—F.W.J. Schelling

FADE IN:

Burmese Jungle. Banks of Salween River. Trail. Dusk. Stuart looks skeptically over Avery's shoulder at the now slightly crumpled photograph of Baptiste and the guerrilla fighter. Avery sits across from him with the Google-Asia printouts and the photo on her lap. She sucks on a Camel-Back hose as Stuart applies sunscreen to her shoulders. They are lingering at an overlook on an otherwise dense jungle trail,a place where the trail forks in two directions.

Superimpose:

Burmese Jungle. Salween River Range.

STUART

I dunno, Ave.

He looks up and around.

It still seems farfetched, you know?

He snaps shut the sunscreen and opens a bottle of water. Avery reads from her printout.

AVERY

'Attention people of the West, people of
the press in lands uncensored. We are the
Vigorous Burmese Student Warriors.
Outcast enemies of an evil regime.
Request your aid.' Etcetera etcetera.
Signed 'Sonny Tun-Tun, VSW leader.'

She smacks the page excitedly and looks up at Stuart. Stuart drains some bottled-water over his head.

STUART

And you think that guy's connected to
Baptiste? And that he's out here
someplace? And maybe, just maybe—

BARRETT

Have we reached the end of the rainbow,
dearies?

He drags himself into the scene.

I say, if the heat is any indication, our
prey must surely inhabit the depths of
hell. Poor fellow.

Simeon arrives behind him, drenched in sweat. A pair of BURMESE PORTERS enter behind them carrying the group's gear, including several large crates of VidaStout beer. Avery stands up and looks toward the mountains with a topographical map in hand.

AVERY

You saw the printout, Stu. Sorbonne gets two hits linked to that posting. Plus, remember what Baptiste said before he bit it?

Stuart tosses Simeon a water bottle.

STUART

No.

Simeon declines the water and yanks out a VidaStout.

AVERY

'In Myanmar there is a young man, a bright light.'

Avery reaches into her bag for a pair of binoculars. Barrett takes the photograph from Stuart.

STUART

Right, but. I mean, A dying philosopher mentions a man in Myanmar. Fine. Google gives us this Sonny Tun Tun guy in Burma. Throw in a photo of Baptiste with a dude in a mask and the initials 'ST' on the back.

(beat)

Don't you think we're forcing it?

Simeon downs a swig. Belches.

SIMEON

Myanmar's what the bad guy's call Burma.

Avery trains the binoculars on something. Barrett flips a coin.

BARRETT

Ahh, the long arm of modus tollens.

AVERY

I see a campfire.

The Porters see where she is looking. They promptly turn and head off back in the direction from whence the group came. Simeon blinks Visine into his eyes.

SIMEON

Look's like the help's clocking out.

Avery turns then turns back. She tosses Stuart the binoculars.

AVERY

I have a feeling about this, Stu. Absurd? Probly. But I'm ready for that. Baptiste was ready for that. The least of these, man. You gotta have faith.

(beat)

Anyway, that fire can't be more than two clicks away.

SIMEON

Clicks?

Avery marches back to their gear and starts divvying things up. Simeon hands Barrett his beer and sets off up the trail.

AVERY

(to Simeon)

Hey Leibniz!

SIMEON

Gotta drain the main vein.

He starts unbuckling his shorts, steps idly onto some leaves, and is suddenly swung into the air, a rope looped taut about his ankle. He screams and waves his arms madly while rocking like a pendulum.

STUART

Holy—

Barrett swigs the beer. Simeon screams again. A branch cracks and he drops in a heap on the trail.

AVERY

Shitzou.

(to herself)

My God.

She and Stuart drop their things and start out toward Simeon. A DOZEN CAMOUFLAGED MEN appear out of the brush with rifles levelled. Barrett drops his beer and raises his arms in a sign of surrender.

¤

Paris. Simone's Office Building. Night. A fifty-dollar bill makes for a sly offering between two fingers. The Janitor looks at it, then looks at Agent Cavell. They are in a dimly lit hallway outside the glass walls of Simone's office suite.

JANITOR

Euros.

Agent Cavell frowns and digs some bills from his wallet. The Janitor stuffs them in his shirt pocket then pulls out his keys. After a quick look over his shoulder he unlocks the door. He turns on the office lights. Cavell punches them off again and closes the door on the Janitor behind him.

Inside, Agent Cavell surveys the scene and pops a stick of gum in his mouth. He snaps on some latex gloves, takes a slow look around and clicks on a penlight. The walls are adorned with an array of inspirational leftist posters (Che, Mao, Sartre) mingled with framed diplomas. There's a Cal Berkley MA in Rhetoric. A small MA in Public Health from a nondescript 'online' program. He squints. At last his light stops on Simone's Sorbonne diploma. "Jean—Luc Baptiste" is listed as "Advisor", with official signature.

He steps over to a large modernist desk—clean as a whistle, save for a pink post-it pad. Even the recycling box is empty. He shines his light on an old globe, then on a SPEK conference program resting proudly against the globe. The SPEK Medal is draped over the globe. He turns his attention to a bookcase behind the desk. His light passes over a row of books, then backtracks and stops on a hardback edition of Das Kapital. *He snaps his gum, then reaches for the book.*

He turns on the desk lamp and opens the book. Inside, a square has been cut out of the pages, and a small black notebook is stowed there. He whistles. He opens the book to find a list of account numbers and entries. He looks across the desk and spots a fax machine. He pulls his phone from his coat pocket and punches a number. As the call goes through he takes a second look at the post-it pad and studies a faint impression left from the last use.

AGENT CAVELL

(to phone)

Hey Howie.

(beat)

No, I figured as much.

(beat)

Well tell Chief to keep his pants on. Looks like we've got a new dog in this fight.

He rubs a pencil sideways across the post-it pad and holds it to the light. "VidaStout" appears.

Just wait for my fax. Then call me when you got something. I have a feeling it may take some doing.

He fingers the post-it. The hallway elevator dings. Agent Cavell looks up. He clicks off his phone. Two SECURITY GUARDS step out of the elevator and into the office. Two flashlight beams land on Cavell's face as he sits nonchalantly on the edge of Simone's desk.

SECURITY GUARD 1

(in French; subtitled)

You! Who are you?! How did you get in here!?

Cavell holds his wrist watch up to the light and checks the time.

AGENT CAVELL

(in fluent French; subtitled)

Four and a half minutes. Mighty slow, gentlemen. Mighty slow.

He flashes his badge quickly (for the show of it) as they approach him.

I'm the security consultant for Dr. Marseilles.

(beat)

She took out a very expensive account with us so as to ensure the total security of this office.

He snaps a bubble, then drops his penlight in his shirt-pocket.

Looks like we have some work to do,
don't we?

The Security Guards look at Agent Cavell then each other awkwardly.

SECURITY GUARD 1

Dr. Marseilles is away in the States.

AGENT CAVELL

That so?

Spits his gum in the trash.

What, another conference?

Guard 1 shuffles and looks uncertainly at Guard 2.

SECURITY GUARD 1

Her research facility.

Agent Cavell absorbs the comment but gives nothing away.

AGENT CAVELL

Jack of all trades I guess. Well, whatever it is, that would explain why she requested my appointment with this office at the present moment. Am I right?

The Guards look at him, and each other, unsure what to do.

You may go, gentlemen.

(beat)

I will have my office send you a list of recommendations in the morning. Goodnight.

The Guards linger in confusion, then turn slowly for the door.

I'll lock-up.

He watches them exit, then looks to the fax machine and back to Simone's account book/post-it. He takes another glance at the recycling bin.

(to himself)

Somebody's pullin the wool over my eyes.

¤

Burmese Jungle. Clearing. Sonny Tun-Tun's Campfire. Night. A log lands on a crackling campfire, sending out a stream of sparks. BURMESE REBELS mill about wearing camouflage shirts and traditional longyis (men's skirts), with rifles nearby. They have tapped into the VidaStout supply. Avery, Simeon, Stuart and Barrett sit on the ground with their hands tied behind their backs and burlap sacks covering their heads.

REBEL 1 approaches Avery, beer in hand, and tears off her head covering. He smiles at her. Pats her on the head.

REBEL 1

Duck.

He does the same for Stuart.

Duck.

And for Barrett.

Duck.

Before finally stopping in front of Simeon, crouching down in mock suspense, and tearing off the burlap.

Goose!

He takes off running around the fire, then collapses to the ground and takes a swig of his beer. The other Rebels applaud and cheer. Avery smiles awkwardly. Barrett wriggles his arms and tries to loosen his hands.

BARRETT

Pray God, these vines aren't sumac.

A man's voice shouts from up a nearby hill, ordering in Burmese. The guards compose themselves. Avery turns and squints into the darkness. REBEL 1 begins cutting loose their hands.

Oh. How very kind.

REBEL 2 doles out portions of rice in wooden bowls. Simeon winces and rubs his ankle. Stuart dumps some of his rice into Avery's bowl. She looks at him. He averts his eyes. She waves shyly at REBEL 1.

AVERY

Sorry. Excuse me. Sir. Hi. Can you understand me?

REBEL 1 points inquisitively at his beer as if to offer her one.

Oh. Um. Actually we came here. See, we heard of a guy.

She eases out the photo and her Google printout.

A, ahh, a Mr. Tun-Tun?

She holds out the photo.

Do you know if—

A hand takes the photo. A man enters the fire circle, hefts a dead chicken to the Rebels, sits down on a stump, crosses his legs, and looks at the photo. This is SONNY TUN-TUN.

Stuart freezes with a spoon of rice before his mouth. He looks at Avery. Sonny Tun-Tun looks at Avery and the others. He hands the photo to Rebel 1 and places his hands on his knees.

SONNY TUN-TUN

(in southern-accented English)

So, you'all friends of the professor's?

¤

Monad Labs. Waiting Area. Night. Elmo Exum strains over a clip-board, pen in hand.

ELMO EXUM

(reading/reacting)

'Medical History?' Ahh hell,

(writing)

Complicated. 'Do you the intended recipient of this organ to qualify as attaining at or below the lowest income level of the US tax bracket?'

Scratches chin.

Well, depends. 'Do you agree to allow the proprietors of Monad Labs, and its affiliates, to utilize your case for the purposes of publicizing public health initiatives worldwide?'

(signing)

Sure, why not.

Elmo lowers the clip-board and reaches for a counter-top bell, dinging it. He looks around.

(loudly)

Okay boys. All set now.

(beat)

I say okay fellas!?

Lab Office. Same time. Guy, a snack-bag of bright orange, triangular chips in hand, observes Elmo Exum on a security monitor. He shakes his head. Henri is at a desk across the room, punching figures into a calculator.

HENRI

(crunching; in French, subtitled)

Doesn't look like a philosopher.

GUY

Look rich?

Guy studies the feed as Elmo mouths a cigar, tries the exit door and finds it locked. Guy tilts his head uncertainly.

Should I put him in the basement?

¤

Sonny Tun-Tun's Camp. Bunkhouse. Morning. A rooster crows loudly. Dawn is breaking outside a rough bunkhouse in which Barrett and Simeon sleep. Stuart is seated on the floor and writing in a reporter notebook. Simeon's leg is elevated. The rooster crows again.

BARRETT

(groggily)

In God's name.

Simeon yawns, shakes his head, stares at the thatched ceiling.

SIMEON

Cock.

Stuart looks over his notebook to the screened windows.

STUART

Kinda nice.

Barrett hauls himself up.

BARRETT

Don't suppose it's calling us to omelets
and toast?

Simeon eases out of bed and hobbles toward the screen-door. Summoning an elevated tone,

SIMEON

Oh thou rosey-fingered dawn whom the
ancients lauded! Must you prod us from
our slumber?

Scratches himself.

This place got a latrine?

He tries the door, then jerks it harder. It doesn't budge. Stuart turns over a fresh page in his notebook.

STUART

Locked.

Simeon leans his head into the door then kicks it. He looks up and presses his face against the screen. He looks down the hill to the campfire site. Rebels are asleep around the smoldering fire. VidaStout bottles are strewn about.

SIMEON

Hey! Hey, rebels!

Shakes the door furiously.

Geneva Convention mean anything to you?!

The rooster crows.

¤

Paris. Facility Maintenance Area outside Simone's Office Building. Pigeons scatter as the lid on a large paper-recycling bin opens. The Janitor pops a gum bubble and holds a grimy hand out to Agent Cavell. Cavell begrudgingly hands him a Euro note, then rolls up his sleeves as he looks at the mess of office paper.

Airplane. A FLIGHT-ATTENDANT offers Simone a glass of wine and a selection of magazines. Simone accepts a copy of Foreign Affairs. *She opens it over her wine and absorbs the satisfaction of seeing a photo of herself accepting the SPEK Medal. Headline reads: "Mind & Body: Simone Marseille's Activist Border-Crossings."*

¤

Burmese Jungle. Day. Avery and Sonny are walking through a wooded area. Sonny holds a rifle. Avery wears one of the longyis. Sonny pushes aside some low-hanging brush. Large birds lurch from the brush ahead of them. Sonny brushes a mosquito from her shoulder.

SONNY TUN TUN

We started organizing in the mid-eighties. I was in the states at the time, studying at Rice. It's how I met Baptiste.

He stops and gestures for Avery to watch her step. A large snake slithers out of their way.

SONNY TUN-TUN

He was visiting the department for a term.

(beat)

Anyway, a letter came to me from some friends. My sister had been jailed.

Avery swats at a mosquito.

AVERY

My God.

Sonny pauses and scans the treetops. Avery, weakening in the heat, eases onto a deadfall. Sonny opens a canteen for her.

SONNY TUN TUN

The military junta in Rangoon was turning up the heat on everyone. I flew home, quietly as I could. The peasant farmers in the countryside were already up against water and grazing issues, so we tried to form a wedge around that. You know, give them a voice.

He looks at Avery's flushed, worn appearance.

SONNY TUN-TUN

You okay?

Avery lists to one side then catches herself.

AVERY

Huh? Yeah. No. I'm good.

(beat)

So were you guys publishing anything? Leaflets? Journal articles?

SONNY TUN TUN

We had an underground newspaper for a while, but the resources were slim. And, well, so was the literacy.

He takes Avery's hand to help her over a small stream.

Before long our members started disappearing. The real crackdown came in '88.

Avery looks at him with interest. Sonny wipes his forehead with a rag.

A few escaped and came back with tales of torture. Their bodies said enough.

He removes a glove from one hand and holds up the hand for her to see. The pinky is missing.

I had my own story to tell.

AVERY

Holy Sh— Sorry, man, it's just—

SONNY TUN TUN

It's okay. But my sister wasn't so lucky.

He stops and quietly levels the shotgun at a large bird on a tall tree-branch.

Dissove to Burmese Rebel Camp. Same time. The echo of a rifle shot cracks across the hillside. Simeon and Barrett look up over their shovels from a ditch they are digging. Rebel 1, a rifle around his shoulder, is monitoring their work. He turns and smiles. Simeon closes his eyes, raises a hand in thought.

SIMEON

Twelve gauge.

Barrett wipes his brow.

You think he wacked her?

Stuart, with a hoe beside him, snaps a photo of Simeon, Barrett, and Guard 1 from a nearby garden plot.

Jungle Interior. Same time. Sonny lowers the shotgun. Slings it over his shoulder and steps forward.

SONNY TUN-TUN

If Western cameras had been in our capitol maybe the rest of the world would have taken notice. But we weren't very sophisticated. Anyway, the jungle meant good cover, a chance to reorganize, strategize, study.

He holds a thorny branch back for Avery.

Called ourselves the Student Democratic Front, and pooled our resources with some of the Shan states in the northeast.

AVERY

So, who were you reading. I mean, Foucault? Habermas? Guttierez?

Sonny laughs a little.

SONNY TUN TUN

Nah. Carter. Maybe Nixon. Of course there's Madison and the *Federalist Papers.* But in a pinch I'd go—

AVERY

Who?

SONNY TUN TUN

Jimmy Carter.

Burmese Rebel Camp. Day. Stuart stands at the entrance to a make-shift camp office. Rebel 2 holds the door open for him. Stuart looks at a large poster of Jimmy Carter tacked to a wall above an old computer. He gestures toward the computer.

STUART

Hey. Alright.

He smiles and makes a typing gesture. Rebel 2 smiles and nods. Points to Stuart's notebook and camera.

REBEL 2

You. You Ted Koppel? You newsman?

Stuart looks down at his camera.

STUART

Huh? Oh. No. Nah. Just a barfly.

He raises the camera to snap a photo of Rebel 2, who puts on a proud face. Stuart steps toward the computer. Repeats his typing gesture.

Internet?

Rebel 2 just smiles and points at Stuart.

REBEL 2

Ted Koppel.

Stuart smiles and nods. He sets down his notebook and checks the cables running from the computer. He follows one across the wall, through the ceiling, and steps outside. He sees a small satellite dish affixed to the roof of the office.

STUART

Now we're talking.

Jungle Interior. Same time. Avery smacks a mosquito on her arm. Sonny walks ahead of her.

SONNY TUN-TUN

He was inspiring I guess. Most of us were originally in political science so—

Avery clutches her stomach, leans into the brush, and vomits. She braces her hands on her knees and spits. Sonny returns with a dead bird.

SONNY TUN TUN

Breakfast?

He drops the bird and crouches down.

You okay?

Avery passes out.

Rebel Camp. Day. Simeon, aloft repairing a rickety windmill tower, turns with wrench in hand to the sound of Burmese yelling. Barrett, sweat-pouring over his hoe in the garden, turns in the direction of the voices. Rebel 1, monitoring Barrett, slings his rifle and takes off running toward the voices. Sonny and a Rebel trot into camp cradling Avery between them.

Stuart gets up from the computer. He shakes Rebel 2, who is dozing in a chair with a VidaStout in hand, and bounds through the door. Sonny and a Rebel approach the office carrying Avery. Stuart looks on in concern and holds the door open for them. They bring her in the office and lay her on a cot. Sonny opens his canteen and puts it to her lips.

STUART

What happened?

(beat)

Ave?

Sonny directs the Rebels in Burmese. One exits. Stuart checks Avery's pulse. Sonny feels her forehead. A Rebel returns with a wet towel. Sonny takes it and lays it across Avery's forehead. Stuart draws a sheet up over her chest. Barrett and Simeon press through the door. Barrett takes one look at Avery, then lurches forward and grabs Sonny by the collar. He screams and pins him against the wall. Rebels yell and shoulder their rifles.

BARRETT

Heartless fool. What in God's name?!

STUART

B!

Rebels yell in Burmese. Stuart throws an arm around Barrett's chest and pulls him back. Simeon pushes a rifle aside and bends down over Avery.

Take it easy B! Take it easy.

Sonny remains against the wall catching his breath. Stuart pats his shoulder then turns to Barrett, then Avery.

Her stomach, man. Remember?

(to Sonny)

Ulcers. Stress. Lost her medication.
Probly just—

Simeon looks into Avery's vacant eyes. Feels the skin on her arm.

SIMEON

Nope.

Stuart turns.

STUART

What!? Whatdayamean—

Simeon carefully checks some bumps on Avery's skin.

SIMEON

There's more.

SONNY TUN-TUN

What vaccinations did you get?

STUART

What!?

SONNY TUN-TUN

Immunizations. Before your trip.

(beat)

The rains were late this year.

Stuart looks at him, then Barrett.

¤

Jungle Interior. Evening. Stuart, Simeon, Rebel 1, and Sonny are out walking in the jungle. Simeon licks a cigarette paper and rolls it into a smoke. Stuart scans the brush.

STUART

Malaria typically hits Sub-Saharan Africa the hardest. Two million deaths a year. Of course, it's also endemic to southeast Asia. And it all goes back to—

Swats a mosquito.

F—these little devils.

Simeon takes a long drag and blows smoke on himself. Sonny tosses Stuart a canteen.

SONNY TUN-TUN

Last year we lost two men. Sometimes, maybe, it can be treated.

STUART

At least prevented, herbally.

(beat)

Do you know the plant?

Simeon, cigarette puffing, steps to the side of their clearing and prepares to take a leak. Sonny nods.

SONNY TUN-TUN

Ampelozizyphus.

SIMEON

Sisyphus?

STUART

(to Sonny)

What does it look like?

Sonny looks at him, brushes a mosquito off his arm, then points to some plants resting between Simeon's legs.

Dissolve to Burmese Rebel Camp. Office. Night. Stuart stands at a make-shift sorting table, working on the plant roots. Sonny and Simeon stand nearby. Barrett is seated on a bench and applying natural aloe to his sunburn. Several bottles of VidaStout rest on the table beside Stuart. The Rebels are conducting a native religious ceremony around the campfire.

STUART

Hey Sim, the mallet?

Simeon flips a mallet and presents it to him, handle-first.

And some mineral water. Thanks.

He begins working the roots and beer into a pulpy blend. Sonny watches with interest.

So, I'm a little rusty, but the trick is to overtake the plasmodium gallinaceum, which is especially vulnerable to parasites. You then take the live yeast and caloric sugars in the stout, and blend them with the quinine in the water.

He holds the mixture up and swirls it around. Barrett dabs aloe on his shoulders.

BARRETT

Ahh yes. The Calcutta Cup.

Simeon rolls a smoke.

SIMEON

Come again, brother?

BARRETT

My vicar used to spout off about it to us lads.

Stuart sets the mixture down on the table and motions for Sonny to add some more mineral water. He nods toward the downhill campfire.

STUART

How do you guys handle it?

Sonny looks to the Rebels around the fire, then back to Stuart.

SONNY TUN-TUN

We chew the leaf. We pray.

Holds up VidaStout bottle.

But this is different.

BARRETT

A shame we didn't procure sponsors from the pharmaceutical industry.

Stuart looks for a moment at his mixture.

STUART

(to Sonny)

Ready?

SONNY TUN-TUN

Ready.

They enter the office. Stuart grabs a pen from the desk, unscrews it for a makeshift straw, and places the cocktail near Avery's lips. Sonny watches with keen interest. Avery coughs and awakes slightly.

STUART

That's right. Easy now.

AVERY

(sucking, delirious)

Least. The least.

Caughs.

Get Sonny, Stu. Baptiste. Sonny. The bright light of—

STUART

Shh. Just drink.

Simeon peaks his head through the door, a cigarette butt in his teeth, and holds up some leftover leaves.

SIMEON

Hey, ah, you guys done with these? Thought B and I might—

Sonny and Stuart keep their eyes on Avery. Simeon nods.

It's cool.

He exits. Stuart helps Avery drink some more. He caresses her forehead.

STUART

(to Sonny)

She's delirious. Don't worry about—

SONNY TUN-TUN

The least of these.

Stuart turns.

STUART

Yeah.

Sonny rests his elbows on his knees. Stuart pulls the straw from Avery's mouth. She eases into sleep. Sonny takes a deep breath.

SONNY TUN-TUN

Baptiste.

Stuart sits on the cot at Avery's feet.

STUART

Baptiste.

(beat)

So, you know.

SONNY TUN-TUN

I know, yes.

(beat, off Avery)

How the mind hungers for the just. Like a famine in the blood.

Stuart eyes him, absorbing it.

STUART

So, is it, is it real then, or just, you know—

SONNY TUN-TUN

Idealistic?

Stuart nods, then places his hand on Avery's.

I know, I'm familiar with idealism.

He stands and looks out the doorway.

And I know it's a dangerous lifestyle.

Stuart looks at him, takes a deep breath, then gets up and steps over to the computer.

STUART

Look, Sonny. I've started an article. Uploaded some photos.

Sonny turns around and faces him.

And before we go I—

SONNY TUN-TUN

Go?

Stuart stops in confusion.

It's impolite for captives to set the terms. Am I right?

STUART

It's just that I think it would be a good idea to—

SONNY TUN-TUN

You want to interview me.

STUART

Yeah.

Avery's eyes open and close again.

Would mean a lot to her.

Sonny reaches for a beer.

SONNY TUN-TUN

There was a French group. Wanted to interview me. Even funded us for a while. Said they wanted to sneak me out to Paris.

STUART

Baptiste?

Sonny shakes his head.

SONNY TUN-TUN

A colleague. Then she discovered I was connected to Baptiste, and that our movement was pro-democracy.

Stuart listens intently. He looks at the Jimmy Carter poster.

That was that. I told myself I'd never trust the West again. Stuart nods, leans forward, rubs his hands together.

STUART

Well, we're here.

Sonny finishes a swig.

SONNY TUN-TUN

So you are.

STUART

And we can't stay, man.

(beat)

But we can tell your story.

Sonny steps over and takes a seat on the floor beside the cot. He holds the beer up to Stuart. Stuart holds it uncertainly.

SONNY TUN-TUN

Right. But it will cost you.

Stuart frowns, then smiles.

¤

VidaStout Warehouse. Shipping Bay. Day. A heavy-set WORKER in VidaStout company coveralls approaches a fax machine. MEN move about with forklifts and dolleys loading crates of VidaStout. There is a sign beneath the fax machine that reads "ORDERS." The Worker tears off a fresh fax and reads.

WORKER

(to himself)

What the—

Yells over his shoulder.

Get the forklift, Bill!

(beat)

And find out what the hell's come of Elmo.

¤

Florida. Bare Republic. Lodge. Kert, naked as a jay-bird, is whistling as he cleans gutters in the hot sun. The back side of Monad Labs, off in the distance, is in his line of view. A flash of white catches his eye. A rope of bed-sheets knotted together drops from a top-floor window of Monad Labs. Kert shades his eyes and flips up the shades on his eye-glasses. The top end of the 'rope' slips from the window and the escape plan collapses in a pathetic heap. Kert shakes his head and rubs a handful of gutter grime on his shoulder (sun-block).

¤

Burmese Rebel Camp. Morning. Simeon finishes turning a bolt on the windmill. He takes a brace off the blades. Wind tosses his hair. The blades begin to turn. The machinery comes to life. A pipe rises and falls rhythmically at the tower's base. Water gushes into the irrigation ditch. Sonny, Barrett, Stuart, and the Guards applaud and cheer. Simeon takes a dramatic bow from atop the tower.

A weak but restored Avery looks on from the hillside where she is planting seeds in the garden along with Rebel 2. Her color has returned. She nods at the scene, smiles, then reaches for Stuart's camera. Stuart and Sonny turn to look her way. Stuart waves as Avery snaps a photo of the scene. Simeon turns around on the tower and pretends to do a trust fall. Avery laughs.

A Rebel suddenly appears from a hillside trail, running into camp. He yells in Burmese and points his rifle toward the sky. Sonny looks skyward and barks orders to his men. The thwack thwack hum of a helicopter sounds. Stuart and Simeon look skyward. Men scatter with their rifles. Rebel 2 rushes to help Avery up and pulls her under some trees.

A Helicopter appears over the treetops and circles around the camp. Sonny looks on from beneath the water tower. He yells at Stuart as Stuart walks out into the open and watches the helicopter. Stuart looks to Sonny, smiles, and points to the underside of the approaching helicopter.

There is a large red cross painted on the bottom of it, and an oversize crate hung on a steel wire. The word "GOODS" is stamped on one side of the crate, the VidaStout logo on the other. The helicopter hovers twenty feet over the ground and begins lowering the crate. Sonny smiles and steps out. Men, confused, begin to reemerge. Avery turns to Rebel 2

AVERY

Looks like you have your health coverage.

REBEL 2

Ehh?

Avery throws an arm around him.

AVERY

Nevermind.

Dissolve to Rebel Campfire. Night. Avery has her arms around two Men as they dance about the fire. She is wearing a Burmese skirt and a crown of flowers. Simeon beats on a congo drum as Sonny fingers a beat-up banjo. Barrett waltzes among the dancing men and the helicopter pilot with a hand-carved flute. Simeon and Barrett have donned the traditional men's skirts. VidaStout bottles are cheered and strewn about. Laughter abounds.

Avery dances her way to the edges of the circle and reaches for a drink. She looks off into the night and sees Stuart standing by the Helicopter. She watches him for a moment, then grabs a second bottle and slinks off into the moonlight. Stuart stands in the field, beholding the beauty around him. Avery approaches him and the view of the stars.

AVERY

Hey doc.

He turns as she wraps an arm over his shoulder and presents him with a beer.

Maybe Plato was on to something after all.

STUART

Huh?

AVERY

C'mon. You know, book seven. When the future guardians finally step out of the cave, the world of shadows, and at last behold the bright light of the forms, the Good.

He takes a drink. Avery hangs on his shoulder.

The truth itself.

(beat)

Maybe.

Stuart gives her a sideways smile. They stand together for a quiet moment.

You think I'm a fool Stu?

He looks at her, puts an arm around her.

STUART

No. No Ave. Why would I—

AVERY

For bringing us here. Chasing this dream of justice, philosophy, global—

She pins her VidaStout bottle against her forehead.

God, man. We're in Burma. Sponsored by a micro-brew. I mean—

Stuart turns her and holds her before him.

STUART

—Ave.

She lowers her eyes from his. He holds her shoulders before him.

I think you're brave, you're bold—

(beat)

—and beautiful.

She looks up into his eyes. He breaks into a smile.

But Sonny's not the least of these.

She gives a teary laugh.

AVERY

I know.

She wipes her eyes.

I know.

STUART

Now, that's not to say we should just—

Avery grabs his face and pulls it toward hers, kissing him. He drops his beer and gathers her in his arms. They stop after a moment and look at each other.

AVERY

I know, Stu.

(touching his face)

We'll sort it all out in St. Augustine.

He looks at her. Nods.

STUART

In St. Augustine.

He picks her up off the ground. She shrieks playfully.

With Elmo.

They laugh. Stuart carries her toward the dark bay of the Helicopter. He sets her down. She pulls him in. Music and laughter carries toward them from the campfire outside.

¤

St. Augustine. Monad Labs. Day. Elmo's Dog (Caesar) is seated on the sandy driveway outside Monad Labs, staring at Elmo's limo. There is a loud thud repeating on the driver's door. The door pops open. Caesar whimpers softly and pants. Elmo's Chauffeur, his mouth gagged, his arms and legs bound, shuffles across the seat toward the door and falls to the ground. He tries to get up.

Washington DC. Office. Day. Howie swivels in his chair at his cubicle desk. He's wearing a headset phone. He unwraps a bright yellow candy, blows on it, tosses it in his mouth, then sets the wrapper on one of the scales belonging to Lady Justice (formerly on Agent Cavell's desk). He studies his computer monitor.

HOWIE

(to phone)

Uh-huh. Wasn't easy, but turns out they're US accounts. The money's coming through a place called, hang on,

Clicks his mouse to open new screen.

Monad Labs.

(beat)

Looks like a bio-tech of some sort. With overseas NGO status, which means we can't touch it.

Typing.

Well, it's unclear. But from there the cash jumps to Paris, Geneva, then, let's see, fans out in small sums around the developing world.

St. Augustine. Bare Republic. Same time. Agent Cavell pulls into the Bare Republic entrance just as Kert is out picking up the newspaper, wearing house slippers.

AGENT CAVELL

(to cell-phone)

Thanks, Howie. I owe you.

DC Office. Howie sets a pile of yellow, orange, and red candies on the scales.

HOWIE

Hey, see your friends in the paper today?

Agent Cavell nods through his window to an approaching Kert. Sees the newspaper.

AGENT CAVELL

(to phone)

Just about to.

He hangs up. He steps out of the car and shows his badge.

KERT

I'll be damned. Got the message after all.

Cavell nods then points to the newspaper.

AGENT CAVELL

Mind if I?

Kert hands him the paper. Cavell opens it, flips it over, and sees a photo of Avery, Barrett and the Burmese Guards digging in the camp's garden. The headline reads: "Stout Scholars Dig Relief Work." There is an insert shot of Elmo holding a VidaStout. The byline reads "Stuart MacPherson."

KERT

Hey, ain't that that philosopher lady?

Cavell looks at him and smiles. He takes off his sunglasses.

AGENT CAVELL

So tell me about your neighbors.

Kert grins at him, then something else catches his eye off Agent Cavell's shoulder.

KERT

What in the hell—

Cavell turns to look. There, desperately hopping his way around the corner up the drive is Elmo's bound and gagged Chauffeur.

Dissolve to St. Augustine Airport. Night. The VidaStout jet touches down on the runway. Stuart, Avery, Barrett and Simeon, all wearing Burmese skirts, push through a set of doors and enter the arrivals terminal. A CROWD OF PEOPLE holding VidaStout placards cheer and applaud. Dale, with a group of PINT-SIZE SCHOLARS AND PARENTS gathered around him, whistles and claps. Avery and Stuart exchange a perplexed glance. Barrett and Simeon look at each other. Barrett bows to the crowd. Simeon trots around slapping high-fives. Dale reaches to shake Stuart's hand.

STUART

Wh—, What—

Dale smiles, pats him on the shoulder.

DALE

Local news did a spot on you guys. Came to Mother T's to interview me and everything.

Hands Stuart the newspaper with their story in it.

Nice dress.

AVERY

News?

DALE

Yeah! What, didn't know you were celebrities?

(beat)

Anyway, I made a few calls, you know, get the troops out.

Stuart looks up from the paper. He smiles awkwardly and hands it to Avery. Barrett signs a few autographs for the locals.

STUART

Elmo see this?

Dale looks over the paper at him and shrugs his shoulders.

DALE

Funny thing, man. Dropped off the panhandle. Not a word.

Stuart studies him.

Yeah. His investors been calling the bar every day all fired up about the story. But they can't find him either.

Stuart looks at Avery.

Curbside. Airport Terminal. Exit doors slide open as Stuart and Avery rush out. Stuart madly hails a taxi.

AVERY

The hospital?

STUART

His liver deal. Had to be. Who knows, maybe it's—

Simeon's Hearse squeals up to the curb beside them, just as Simeon and Barrett exit the terminal.

AVERY

(to Simeon)

—Your car, dude.

The passenger door swings open in front of Avery. Smoke billows out. She looks at the others, then bends down to look inside. Kert, naked, is behind the wheel, sucking on a hookah hose. He waves.

KERT

Hey there, young miss.

AVERY

(stunned)

Um, howdy Kert.

KERT

Hop on in. Regards from Jimmy Cavell.

She stares at him, dumbfounded. He waves her in.

Lickety-split now. Injustice awaits.

Avery looks from Kert over to Stuart. She enters the car. The others follow. The hearse peels out.

En route. Stuart is leaning forward between Kert and Avery. The hookah hose is making the rounds, only it ain't tobacco. The hearse is hauling.

AVERY

(to Kert)

So, Cavell told you to tell us that someone we might know might at present be held by your neighbors against his will?

KERT

You bet. And that's classified.

Stuart hoists Avery the hookah hose. She takes a puff, coughs, looks suspiciously at the hose. Kert straightens the hookah.

Oh yeah. Hope you don't mind. My glaucoma's a bitch at night.

From the back of the vehicle.

SIMEON

My turn.

Barrett grabs it from Stuart and sucks hard.

STUART

So why doesn't Cavell just bust in there and sort it out himself?

KERT

Beats me. Something about jurisdiction I gather.

He executes a sharp turn. Avery looks out the window and takes a deep breath. Simeon exhales and lays his head back blissfully.

SIMEON

I like the way you ride, Kert.

Dissolve to Bare Republic Entrance. Night. The Hearse pulls in. They all step out slowly. Simeon and Barrett are especially off balance. Kert leads the way around the front of the car and points to some distant woods on the edge of their property. The group gathers around in front of the headlights. Crickets chirp.

KERT

There's the backdoor.

They all look. Kert steps over to the porch.

STUART

Any thoughts?

Kert comes back with a crate of items. He drops it in front of them and reaches into it.

KERT

We gathered what we could to help out.

(beat)

Let's see. Headlamp.

Tosses it to Avery.

Bolt cutters.

Lobs them to Stuart.

Survival kit.

Plants it in Barrett's hands.

And, pellet pistol.

Tosses it against Simeon's chest.

They all stand still, a bit mystified. Fog rises around them. Kert looks at them with his hands on his hips. He sniffles. Avery slowly puts on the head-lamp. She takes a few steps forward in the direction of the woods. Stuart watches her. She tilts her head to the stars for a moment, flicks on her headlamp, then faces the group.

AVERY

Well, boys. What goes up, must come down, right?

Barrett and Simeon look at each other, then nod to Avery.

So let's finish this.

Stuart smiles. Barrett swallows hard. Simeon raises the pellet pistol in the air and cocks it. Avery nods solemnly then turns to head for the woods. The others start out behind her. Simeon slaps Kert on the ass and gives a thumbs-up over his shoulder.

SIMEON

Keep the engine warm, brother.

Kert jingles the hearse keys and watches them go.

KERT

Careful now. Place is teeming with biohazard.

Grounds of Monad Labs. Night. Avery's lamp shines on a tall wire fence, capped by three feet of barbed wire. Stuart drops to his knees and begins cutting an opening. Barrett opens the survival kit, pulls out a small canister, and starts spraying himself. Avery looks at him. He sprays her neck.

AVERY

Hey!

BARRETT

(sotto)

No need to thank me, my dear.

Stuart steps back from the fence. Avery kicks the hole open. They all crawl through, then run to the back side of a cement wall, just beyond the reach of floodlights. Avery crouches and monitors the movement of the lights. She pats Stuart on the back and points to a pair of mopeds parked against another wall. Simeon slinks off, then whistles. Stuart and Avery turn to see him standing beside a loose air vent. They hustle over.

Inside Monad Labs. Same time. Guy and Henri are eating popcorn and watching late night comedy on an old TV. There is a corridor behind the mesh/glass interior window of the lounge. A steam vent pops open over a hallway. Simeon's skirt, then flabby back with pistol tucked in waistband eases down through it. He drops to the floor and helps the others down.

A pair of DOBERMANS perk their ears within the office. Guy and Henri laugh at Jim Carey's entry on the comedy set.

Avery turns her attention to a facility map on the hallway wall. She points to a sector and interprets.

AVERY

Surgical and Storage Suite, Basement

They turn and head down the hallway in the direction opposite the lounge. One of the Dobermans growls, the other drools. Henri feeds them some popcorn.

Avery comes down a staircase and rounds a corner with the others, then another corner. She stops in front of a fogged-up glass door marked "Surgery/S." Avery rubs the rest of it with her sleeve. "Surgery/Storage." She looks at Stuart.

Outside. Monad Labs Entrance Area. Same time. Simone steps out of a taxi, throws her purse over her shoulder, and heads for the entrance. She sees Elmo's limo badly hidden in some nearby brush and shakes her head. Caesar lies on the ground beneath the limo's trunk. He growls. Simone punches some numbers on a key-pad and waits for the door to open.

Inside Lab. Same time. A gurney blasts open the doors of the surgical suite and Avery rushes in past Stuart and Simeon. It is a large dark room, clouded with cold, refrigerated air. Simeon flips on the lights. They all stop and look around. Simeon approaches a table in the center of the room on which a large tarp is draped over something. Avery waves a hand through the fog.

AVERY

Why's it so cold?

A voice sounds from the far corner of the room.

ELMO EXUM

Exactly!

Stuart and Avery turn in surprise.

Lab Entrance/Hallway. Same time. Dobermans lurch from the lounge and nearly collide with Simone as she passes through the entryway beside the lounge. They bound down the hallway on the trail of the Philosophers, their clawed feet sliding on the tiled floor.

Surgery/Storage Suite. Stuart and Avery can barely make out a hospital bed through the fog. Stuart identifies the fleshly face and Hawaiian shirt-collar of Elmo Exum. He is half-elevated on the bed with a thin hospital sheet thrown over him, and one hand handcuffed to a nearby rail.

STUART

Mr. Exum?

Avery studies Stuart, then Elmo. Elmo squints to try and make out their faces. The cold fog disperses before them. Simeon pulls back the tarp covering the object in the center of the room.

ELMO EXUM

Brother Mac? What in God's good name—

Simeon beholds a half-naked man encased in a clear refrigerated chamber.

SIMEON

Is this guy doing here?

Avery and Stuart turn their heads. Avery steps over to the encased body. Fog is streaming from it. Convenience store ice encases it. She looks down at the face of Jean-Luc Baptiste. She stares at him, stunned. Stuart joins her. He observes a set of black-markered markings on Baptiste's chest and stomach—a kind of road-map for organ removal incisions. Barrett vomits into a nearby sink.

ELMO EXUM

My donor. So they tell me.

AVERY

(sotto)

Baptiste.

Elmo rattles his handcuff.

ELMO EXUM

Only, we seem to be tied up in trade negotiations.

(beat, to Avery)

Howdy, miss.

Stuart looks to Elmo, then Avery.

Hallway. Dobermans round the first hallway turn, barking madly.

Outside. Caesar perks his ears and barks.

Inside. The barking of the Dobermans carries into the surgical suite.

SIMEON

Oh boy.

Avery continues staring at Baptiste's face.

AVERY

(sotto)

The least of these.

Stuart rushes over to Elmo and clamps the handcuff chain in his bolt-cutter. The sound of Simone shouting at Henri and Guy outside carries with the barks down the hallway toward them. Barrett hangs uneasily over the sink.

BARRETT

The Reds.

Elmo rubs his wrist and rolls his feet to the floor.

ELMO

Train's a coming, young people. Ain't no time to be lost.

Simeon bounds to a door on the far side of the room. He busts the lock with a fire extinguisher and opens it. Stuart drops his bolt-cutters and hauls Elmo into a wheelchair. Avery stands over Baptiste. Tears form in her eyes.

STUART

Ave!

He lets go of Elmo and hustles to grab Avery.

C'mon, Ave. We have to leave him. C'mon.

Avery turns then pulls back. She reaches into her skirt pocket and slaps a 'Peace' button on top of Baptiste's container. Barrett wheels Elmo through the door, with Stuart and Avery close behind. Simeon, holding the door, levels his pistol and fires at the Dobermans as they tear into the room. The dogs yelp and slide across the floor. He shucks the pistol in his skirt-band and darts from the room.

They fly down another hallway, searching for an exit. Stuart takes over wheelchair duty as Barrett tries a series of locked doors.

ELMO EXUM

(to Stuart)

Any luck in Asia, son? I had to cover for your mishaps in France, you know. Lord, now there was a—

Stuart rushes on, looking about for safe passage.

STUART

I think you'll be pleased, sir.

Barrett throws up his hands in frustration as there is no exit to be found.

BARRETT

A labyrinth! Not even an idle—

Simeon halts in thought.

SIMEON

—window.

Shakes his head.

Damn.

ELMO EXUM

(to Stuart)

Pleased? Don't coddle me now. Just cause
I'm a poor invalid don't—

STUART

VidaStout never bluffs, sir.

Simeon stops at a short hallway off their own. There is a staircase leading to an exit door.

SIMEON

People!

He points toward a door. The Dobermans are closing in. The team hauls Elmo up the stairs and bounds through the door.

Outside. Lab Entrance Area. Nearing Dawn. Elmo's wheelchair bounces out onto a grassy patch beside the edge of the driveway. The Doberman's spring out the exit close behind them. Caesar darts from his post and flies between the team and the Doberman's. He holds them off with a menacing growl. Henri, Guy, and Simone fly through the door and stop short beside the Dobermans.

Simone, flustered, takes a long bitter look at the Philosophers. Avery, with hands on her hips, returns the look. Crickets chirp. One by one, Avery, Stuart, Barrett, and Simeon cross their arms with resolve and look sternly at Simone. Elmo looks from one group to the other, uncertain.

ELMO

Okay then—

SIMONE

(to Avery)

So.

AVERY

So.

One of the Dobermans snaps at Caesar. Barrett deftly hoses it down with some mace from his survival kit. Henri steps forward in alarm and Barrett points his canister at him. Simeon looks at Guy and taps his pistol.

(to Simone)

All this as sick as it seems?

Across the driveway a set of headlights flare on. Agent Cavell steps in front of them and pops a bubble between his teeth.

AGENT CAVELL

'Fraid so.

Everyone turns in surprise.

SIMONE

('relieved')

Agent Cavell, darling. Thank God. Once again your erstwhile compatriots are interfering with our research.

Cavell forces a tight smile then shakes his head.

AGENT CAVELL

'Fraid not.

(to the philosophers)

Hello gang.

(beat; to Simone)

Thought I might buy 'em a drink, actually.

ELMO EXUM

First sensible idea I heard all night.

Avery looks uncertainly at Agent Cavell. Simone takes a sharp breath.

AGENT CAVELL

Yeah. Least I could do, you might say.

He steps toward the group.

Since it all started on a point about *the least.*

He eyes Simone.

Didn't it Dr. Marseilles?

He tosses Simone his own copy of Foreign Affairs. *He meets Avery's gaze.*

Yep. Sick is the word for it. Sick, then dead, then conveniently out of the picture.

BARRETT

Appalling. You've outdone yourself, Simone. Once, you and I, the starcrossed children of love and peace, now—

Simone throws her hands to her hips.

SIMONE

This is—

AGENT CAVELL

—absurd? Thought of that too.

SIMONE

(to philosophers)

Baptiste, if you must know, betrayed his own dream long ago. Isn't that right Agent Cavell?

Avery turns in alarm.

AGENT CAVELL

Not exactly. But that's classified.

SIMONE

(growing desperate)

He alienated everyone! We're just giving him a second chance to be useful.

AGENT CAVELL

Looks to me like you're sportin' the ring of Gyges.

Avery levels a confused gaze at him. He pulls out The Republic *from his coat and lobs it to Simone.*

Book Two.

Elmo points in approval.

ELMO EXUM

Oh hey, that's good shit, boy.

Simone turns in anger from the scene.

SIMONE

How dare you lecture me on justice! You've no idea what—

A shotgun cocks out in the darkness. A Police Officer steps into the light behind Agent Cavell and points a shotgun at Simone. It is the same Officer Simeon met in his embarrassing traffic intervention. She winks at Simeon. He nods his chin and levels his pistol at Henri and Guy.

AGENT CAVELL

What it means to fight for justice?

(beat)

Oh, I've some idea.

He tosses Avery a pair of handcuffs and nods to Simone. Avery looks at Agent Cavell, then down at the handcuffs. Elmo scratches Caesar's ears.

ELMO EXUM

Well, damn. The boy don't bluff.

AGENT CAVELL

(to Avery)

Your case, Dr. Meir.

Avery looks at him, then at Simone. She pauses, shakes her head. She throws the handcuffs to the Police Officer and walks toward Simone. The Officer wrangles the cuffs and looks to Cavell with concern. He considers the moment, then waves her off. The Officer lowers her shotgun. Simeon lowers his pellet gun. Stuart watches Avery as she stops before Simone.

AVERY

Do you know what Saint Augustine wanted more than anything?

Simone curses at her in French.

Do you know?

Guy raises his hand uncertainly. Henri kicks sand at him.

A goddamn second chance. That's what.

(beat)

So this is how this is gonna go, honey. Okay by you, Homeland?

Agent Cavell snaps his gum.

AGENT CAVELL

We'll sort it out.

Avery locks eyes with Simone and points to the door.

AVERY

You go and give Baptiste a second chance. A third chance. A fourth. Give everything he's got to every poor, disenfranchised soul in the world. You follow?

Simone scowls, a little off balance. Avery levels a pointed finger at her.

And if you take one bit of credit, if you play the 'activist' card at any conference ever again I will happily arrange a long sabbatical of immersion work for you with my friends in Burma.

Avery turns away. Stuart nods to her. Guy looks to Henri in amazement. Henri shrugs his shoulders. Guy attempts to give Barrett a hug of gratitude. Stuart takes Avery by the hand.

STUART

So whaddya say, Elmo. How bout that liver?

Elmo pushes up out of the wheelchair and starts ambling toward his car. He pats his side.

ELMO EXUM

Due time, Brother Mac. Due time. Let's go see if we can't give the one I got another drink.

(beat)

C'mon Caesar.

Stuart grins. Agent Cavell smiles. Avery lays her head on Stuart's shoulder. Simeon raises his pistol in the air and shouts over a barrage of pellet fire.

SIMEON

Wolverines!

Dissolve to Mother T's Bar. Entrance. Day. Avery looks fondly out over the block surrounding the bar, then upward to a familiar billboard. She holds the door to the bar open for Kid 1 and Tommy, eyes the billboard. Billboard dissolves into the following quote:

"Pessimism of the intellect, optimism of the will"

—*Romain Rolland*

She lets the door close, and stares into the bar through the large window. The Philosophers are enjoying a good time with the Pint-Size Scholars. Agent Cavell and Dale are at the bar pouring apple juice. Simeon is schooling some kids in scrabble.

AVERY (Voice Over)

It's hard to say where all this ends. Or where it all began. Some would call it fate, others choice, or maybe just plain foolishness.

Barrett is telling stories to a circle of kids. Elmo holds one kid on his lap.

But once upon a time there was this small group of philosophers and a rather resourceful barfly slash, well, citizen. Together we tried to do some good. Failed mostly. Utterly you might say. But hey, we did it together. A stout, far-from-perfect few.

Stuart plays slapjack with a young girl. Avery smiles, then turns toward the sidewalk and spots the Homeless Man. He's got his nose in The Republic. *She smiles at him but he doesn't register her goodwill. She sets off on a stroll.*

Dissolve to Convention Center Lecture Hall. Avery stands behind a podium with the SPEK medal draped about her neck. She has a trimmer haircut and looks restored. A sign on the front of the podium reads "SPEK, 2011" with an image of Baptiste in the background. An audience of PHILOSOPHERS fill the room.

AVERY

So here's to you, to us, the least of these in our own right. And here's to you, St. Augustine, for giving me, well, a second chance.

(to herself)

Does this make any sense?

(mic picks up)

A second chance.

She raises the medal, smiles awkwardly. Some philosophers grimace. Others show signs of solidarity. Camera flash.

Music:

"Knockin' on Heaven's Door,"

Bob Dylan

ROLL CREDITS

Acknowledgments

My sincerest thanks to the many good souls and communities who model for me a genuine devotion to philosophy, justice, and the gracious mirth through which we may sometimes laugh at ourselves. Without implicating anyone per se in the tomfoolery of this project, the fun would not have been indulged without the whimsical sagacity and fellowship of wayfaring friends, including (but not limited to): Matt Chandler, Ian Deweese-Boyd, Michael Kelly, Jeffrey Hanson, David Curcio, Alison Lutz, Jason Wirth, and Bernie Freydberg. I am especially grateful to Richard Kearney for reminding me of philosophy's fundamental kinship with the literary imagination, to Cheston Knapp and Joshua Hren for exercising the literary craft so well, and to my wife, Christen, for embodying that form of the good we all so desperately need. I owe you folks a round of VidaStout.

Through **Rota Fortunae Press** we publish works that dramatize the wheel of fortune at play in the world; pieces that work out the perennial problems of fate, faith, and freedom in the flesh of fiction; works that fate new forms into the world of books.

31998114R00139

Made in the USA
Lexington, KY
04 May 2014